TANGLED IN THE WIRE

Francis Gregory Wood

OTHER WORKS

Crusts & Crumbs Living Legends Limited 1996
Starved For Sanity Brass Bull Press 1997
The Chord File Fortithings Press 1998
Exquisite Minutia FraidiCat Pages 1999
Another Place & Time FraidiCat Pages 2000
Enchanted Words Wulfyre Papers 2008
Hand-Carved Curiosities Wulfyre Papers 2009
The Collected Poetry Of Zackery Crighton Whitewulf
Wulfyre Papers 2010
A Dog's Life: Journeys With Zackery
Wulfyre Papers 2012
Wulfyre Traveling Show Wulfyre Papers 2013
Seventeenth Segment Wulfyre Papers 2014
New Wine From Old Bottles Wulfyre Papers 2015
By These Stripes Wulfyre Papers 2016
After Two & Twenty Wulfyre Papers 2017
Against The Black-Chrome Sun Wulfyre Papers 2018
Founding Wulfsgate Wulfyre Papers 2019

TANGLED IN THE WIRE
Francis Gregory Wood

www.wulfyre.com

just as he mustered the courage
to once again lift his head
above the surface of
that pool of muck
- they fired yet another shot
in his direction
- to which he simply
smiled the lunatic grin that
had become his stock in trade
- as he mumbled to himself
that they were gonna have
to try a hell of a lot harder
than they had so far
- if their intent was to
shut him down or
silence the voice
he'd worked so freaking hard
all these years
- to turn into the one
he used now

FRONTISPIECE

Within the incurable romantic's lexicon, for a smithy of words or an orator of lines there lurk innumerable possibilities of how to apply Love's vocabulary. But this process only achieves success if at least two people read or hear and absorb those words simultaneously. For only then can the results reach credibility without lapsing into the morass of meaningless or silly or trite.

My work over the preceding almost thirty years explores the best and worst of human survival as depicted through the many aspects of loving relationships, displayed from myriad viewpoints. Oblique enough by purpose for causing one to need to think a bit about the processes, yet adding enough functionability to allow virtually anyone a more-than fleeting glimpse into the instinctual secrets hiding inside what passes for Love.

Which by extension is integral to actualizing ones life or living. But sometimes of the direst necessity, my sentiments are not couched in trappings either that soft or in the least tender. As there simply are seminal occasions when no words carve so well as those which are launched off the tip of a blood-tempered blade. Often in the midst of a magnificently thundering emotional or literal storm.

But accepting the truths of and dealing with any events or situations in which one finds one's self doesn't hurt that long or badly once one stands and squarely faces them. Allowing for rather effortlessly side-slipping into one of the multiple soul-comforting parallel realities we've each tucked away in darkened un-secured recesses of our psyches for just such emergencies, eventualities or indulgences.

From embracing the rawest energy of the raging inferno which heralds a new Love affair, to the tender care and feeding of more long-practiced souls basking in the glow of the ember-banked pyre which represents a mature continuing union - it's all touched on along the path somewhere in my rambles. Even the specter of ones own mortality or worse, that of our closest tribe members is not that dark and daunting when viewed in the rarified spectrum of this amazing Light Of Love.

Many dramatically tumultuous years transitioning from There to Here have freed me from the mediocre constraint of offering only nice or pretty or fanciful shavings carved from the tree of life by a chiseler's pen. And the craftsmanship I've strop-honed to razor's edge over this lifetime of my own unstaunched bleeding supports the sheer audacity to only compose or construct work which enlightens as it entertains, and vice versa.

No scribbler worth his or her meager ration of the preciously limited resource of salt required for self-preservation can help but live in sheer, utter, perpetual awe of the incredible magnitude of literary and theatrical richness surrounding the all-consuming subject of Love which has previously been scribed down, scripted out or heart-emoted upon The Continuum's innumerable stage boards.

At risk of exposing glaring naivety, I nonetheless insist that there is room for such as-yet undiscovered, grass-roots, home-grown, hand-carved curiosities as mine to hold a certain allure, charm or entertainment value. Intrinsically you also know this too, as that's why you are Here now, plowing through and perusing whatever glints of insight are to be found in this humble document. And participating in my little dust-up in whatever manner or degree which suits you.

MIrrorIng the never-wavering life-long mission of my stalwart character Michael-Eli Long - who you will either grow to Love or loathe, my intent has always been to provide such valued assistance I may accidentally possess with someone's own evolution toward becoming a bit more adept at loving. Thereby at being reciprocally but exponentially loved in return. But again the process only works when I'm privileged to help even two others gain some rare insight into how to better thrive.

Therefore not peering too very deeply into the rather average and/or mundane machinations of, but more to a fuller overall appreciative view of the engaging day-to-day functions required for living a life. In another phraseology not just being physically well, but up to one's fullest emotionally intellectual potential to do and be – somehow more.

Any benefit to be had from what's here is still of some benefit all being said in my singularly-concerted estimation. Whether it's for the common good or in hopes that at least those two persons previously mentioned might say to themselves: "Hey, some guy out there in The Ether cared enough to offer us a piece of his ever-loving soul, for Continuum's sake! So let's give it a fair bit of a go, at least far enough to test his theory."

So. *Tangled In The Wire* began as two stand-alone dramatic or staged readings, each for the same seven characters. With a short story to be read in between instead of a more traditional intermission, they were originally intended to comprise an evening-length live entertainment. But after adding a bit more interweaving material these three pieces became a much more contiguous telling of my intended tale.

Hopefully thereby artfully presenting a richer and more complete tapestry of the story I've felt compelled for a number of years to share with anyone who wanders in to contact with it during their rambling journeys.

All precipitated from my 2013 solo-performance work *Wulfyre Traveling Show. Against The Black-Chrome Sun* was written in 2018 as a stand-alone two-act play. *Founding Wulfsgate* is another staged reading penned in 2019, delving further into the characters as a prequel to *ABCS. By These Stripes* is a complete story on its own composed by my alter-ego Zackery

Crighton Whitewulf in 2016. As it provides deep background details not shared elsewhere to how this saga may have begun in the now-misty days of one possible history, it is positioned between the others here as a bridge from Then to Now.

Oh, speaking of writing styles. A side note as explanation for my readers in this Here and Now: the bookend performance pieces are presented in their close-to original, easy to follow, reading-script format by choice. This to allow those with the same sort of live-art bent I share to enjoy a bit of the feeling of having participated in, or to at least have seen and heard them in a live theatre environment, just as I always intended.

And dependent upon inclination and orientation, you may or not notice numerous references to wine and its rather copious consumption are peppered throughout my work by some characters. That is entirely fitting in context as that to those of us who are appreciative imbibers of this wondrous libation it is every bit as alive and sustaining as the very life-blood flowing through our veins.

While to adult beverage or not and if so to what extent are of course conscious personal choices, there's much to be said for its joyous enjoyment when employed per my imagery in a glorious red rain of liberation.

And so, in the beginning were the words with which to write or die trying. Those efforts have so far produced fourteen volumes of free-verse poetry, a novel-length prose poem, three one-man shows, a two-act play, a couple of short stories and the volume here to round out the current collection.

Heart-felt appreciation and undying devotion to each one who has supported my far-flung creative endeavors over the course of that which passes for my writing career, or whatever folderol this mélange has been thus far. None of what's perhaps been accomplished, would have dare even been dreamed of, much less attempted, without you having believed in and encouraged me to exceed my oh-so-limited reach and grasp.

The amazing technical skills and wondrous artistic expertise granted to my eager employ and liberally applied by those who have participated in my pursuit of these long strange adventures is phenomenal and profoundly humbling. The success of anything achieved at this juncture was only possible because of me being allowed to stand on your strong shoulders in order to enable a continuous reaching for the stars.

Welcome to this little corner of Here. Should it not feel too cozy or much like your old homeplace it's because you have been successfully shifted outside of your neutral or comfort zone. Which all artists nefariously have as an ulterior motive. Enjoy this little romp through those very stars with me or not as you wish my darlings.

But I have hopeful suspicion you won't be able to help yourselves. For I will get to you way down where you actually live after a while, as morbid curiosity and the desire to further emotional evolution both spring from the same poetic loins. Advantage me, as that part of both you and me are already in cahoots.

From this point on you need only grab your empty glass and wade with me into La Riviere Du Vin Rouge which never runs dry. Then just lean into the current of whatever this is or perhaps is not, take my hand and off we'll go. I'm excited for you, as there are always rather delightfully interesting twists, turns, switchbacks and surprises encountered whenever one dares to meander down my paths. And it isn't always only about blood and thunder.

But fair warning: you WILL become tangled in the wire.

DRAMATIS PERSONAE

TRANSIT -
I am your commentator, interpreter and even tour guide for this evening so to speak. Situated outside the cast, I am really more a part of you the audience. I also voice the myriad unspoken or behind-the-scenes emotions, thoughts and reactions the characters may or may not choose or be allowed to act out. I offer insight where required and also bring to life what would otherwise be only rather unbearably dry blocks of stage directions in a script.

MICHAEL -
I am the new voice. A mostly self-made expositor and lay-philosopher, displaced from both my own space and time. I have strived to learn every life-lesson offered by all of my mentors and experiences to the very best of my abilities. Though most probably one of the last word-slingers designated by The Keepers, I am sometimes still unsure of my worth as a writer able to cause real and lasting change. I am however a skilled spoken-word artist who maintains my lifelong mission of simply offering others the opportunity to enjoy a better life.

ELI -
I am Michael's alternate, his Other, his alter-ego and perhaps even his unexplored shadow side. I am the power behind the words credited to him. Also the rather playfully perpetual thorn in Michael's side, who delights in messing with his thoughts and emotions. The consummate writer, producer, director, stage

manager and technician for all theatrical endeavors. The behind the scenes part of Michael's mind, somewhat freed to be a cheerleader for the acting company. Most often I do a ghost-like mime thing none but Michael is able to see, though they seem to often feel my presence.

ZACKERY -

I am the ancient progenitor and leader of myriad journeys toward applying Love's Magic as Lead Guide and Fixer for The Keepers, if modesty permits me to so say. A fierce protector and promoter of human-kind's relationships, I am actually just the rather tired teacher who only wants to know that at least one of my students has "made good". Understanding how philosophy influences life has made me sort of a natural-born historian. Michael's biggest fan. And I am now as forever most importantly, Sienna's life-mate.

SIENNA -

I am Zackery's soul-mate. And the one who has immodestly been called The Higher Reason by those in my tribe. Also the long-standing artistic force of nature who causes even the very colors to thrive. My enduring passion or foremost mission is keeping the daily lives of those I love from overwhelming what masquerades for sanity in the insane surroundings of the Now in which we find ourselves. It has been said that I am a true example of both The Warrior Princess and Mother Goddess archetypes, fully believing in the power of applying liberal doses of romance to make everything work as it should.

SOPHIA -

I am as forever the watcher, the overess and perhaps something of a guardian. An ancient guide and protector of all those who've been assigned to or taken under my charge. Who reveals scant little of my inside self, believing it is the ultimate sign of weakness. Brought into being at a time long forgotten as professional caretaker and coach of Zackery and Sienna as well the rest of humanity. I possess strong organizational and procedural gifts, and understand the options of when to use or withhold these skills as necessity and judgment dictate. I am ad hoc manager of our acting company.

ELISE -

I am modesty aside, the almost perfect live-theatre actress and production assistant. Who has absorbed the most subtle nuances of this indescribable acting craft from every source with which I have come into contact my entire life. Though I've not had or gotten to yet start over as often as many others, I was still hand-chosen by Sophia. I expertly do what, where, when and how as needed. Knowing and applying the how-to's of making meaningful art has allowed me the confidence to 'disarm' audiences into believing what is told or shown them, despite my relatively young age. I simply adore being a part of the theatre. The stage is all.

PROLOGUE

Eli ever the unseen shape-shifting Other, keeps silent witness balanced in the rafters high above the crumbling stage boards as Michael moves toward a sidewall rip in the ancient deteriorating canvas show tent. Then steps out into the seemingly endless desert, where thunderheads loom rather darkly on the far southwestern horizon.

Breathing in that fleetingly glorious flare surrounding a new version of dawn. This surely having everything to do with the peculiar struggle for dominance between those timeless lovers Light and Dark, as a black-chrome sun rises over The Badlands to show what changes the next thousand years hold. In almost a whisper, Eli says:

"Wake now dearest brother."

Michael startles aware still in his highback leather chair, yet not entirely rousing from the recurrent dream or nightmare he can't quite wrap a clear memory around.

He glances across the double kneehole desk in that out-of-the-way backstage nook of the still nearly-new theatre at Eli leaning against the wall with a sheath of papers in one hand and his perennial wineglass in the other.

Reclaiming his own goblet from its accustomed resting place near at hand and taking a goodly gulp, he declares with more than just a note of angst in his voice:

"Eli. That wasn't a bit funny, leaving us with nothing worth saying out there tonight. You'd sworn the rewrites were good this time, but it was all just crazy words. A horrible sham, what we gave them. Does that mean like it seems, that you've given up and quit on both The Wulfsgate Players and *Against The Black-Chrome Sun* ?"

"Hold there a second Michael. I expected such from you and have new notes here. And you aren't going to dump all over me yet again because I don't use my own voice on stage. As you know I don't care that no one but you can see or hear me, as if I'm not quite real. And I don't need that kind of connectivity or brand of validation as badly as do you.

"But your adlibbing of forgotten lines doesn't help this misguided messiah show thing we're doing. Which by the way was entirely your bright idea to begin with."

"Okay Eli settle. Because while I won't even pretend to understand your over reactive feelings, yes I do know that yours are the lovely words we get to speak out there every night. And that those same words are all we have with which to give ourselves away, make a valid point, share the truth or earn an almost sustaining income."

"That's all well and good Michael, but this is about

how you've begged and whined at me to feed you more and more of my lovely lines all these years since the most recent Someday came and The Dark mostly went away. Yet I still get blamed when you screw up the delivery.

"It's as if I'm expected to miraculously work your errant words and spastic gestures into the script on the fly, so they not only make sense but even almost seem natural. And it's never the others, just you.

"Why is that you bumbler? Did you learn nothing about stagecraft from Zackery and Sienna all those eons you studied under them back in your Wulfyre Traveling Show days before everything changed?"

"See here Eli you scribbler. What you've described the real pros call backstage production, and that's exactly what you signed on for back when you reawakened in my head following that same Someday you mention. So once and for all, let's get some facts straight right now.

"Though you're writing for more than just me now, it's still mostly my speeches. But you don't own any options, opinions or inalienable rights here at Wulfsgate. As *ABCS* was supposed to be an 'us' deal all the way along."

"Oh Michael what wonderful bull you do say when coming up with your own words. But it's not my fault when a performance goes badly, for my work's top-notch stuff.

"And I've got all my papers and both hands full writing new lines fast enough to make you come across like more than the broken down, washed up, cracker-croaking snake oil salesman you once were. Or still are."

"Oh well played, but again Eli you prove my point. You're here specifically to pen incredible lines which make me and the rest sound so fabulous out there every night, without having to utter a single blasted word out loud yourself. Seems to me you got the easier part, by not having to deal with greasepaint, bright lights and what-not.

"And as I don't write these lines anymore it's become my expert abilities which sell your work, as I've got total believability. So you're just going to suck it up and power on through to the bitter end buttercup, as that's the stopping-point in this particular discussion."

"Really Michael? Oh I don't think we're done discussing yet big boy. In fact we're only getting started, as there's a list. For instance: Just how delusional should I allow you to become about yourself? And how dare you come at me with that 'make you do it' load of clap-trap?

"Look. If you've still got enough live brain cells left to understand, despite all the wine swilling we do - and that's a huge if - pride in Art as both written and spoken language is why I set down these words. And not because some freaking idiot thinks he can force me to do so."

"Well now isn't that special, little man? But Eli as viewed from the point of your own exquisitely flawed judgment, it seems that old catchphrase has reared its weary head once again. And it's a line you didn't write by the way, which goes:

"I brought you into this world and can take you back out. Any time any where, by my decision or whim. You're either with me or without me purely as I wish. The others say they've got my back, so I'm not the least bit worried at what'd happen if you were silenced in me once again."

"So that's the bottom line according to Michael Magnificent, huh? Okay then bring it on you prancing play-actor. Come on fancy pants do it, I dare you. And bring all you got. But just don't push me too far, Jack.

"Because remember, the select and delete commands under the drop-down edit box would clear all the freaking files. And fix your cute little red Radio Express wagon right up, real quick-like."

"And yours right along with mine Eli, you posturing wordsmith. Not to mention that we'd be totally screwing over what and to whom we've committed Here. So mister big mouth, say whatsoever you will. Cause we both know bloody-well you don't have either the nerve or lack of ego to obliterate your scriptwork, and by default leave all of us with nothing to tell an audience.

"Especially since you also know what rewards good shows could reap from well informed attendees with discretionary income who also just happen to like both insightful poetry and free-flowing wine."

"Just listen to yourself Michael. The slight possibility of gaining financial support from some unknown, wealthy, drunken patrons is the only card you're going to leave in play? If it's not about us sharing The Wulfyre and The Magic Of Love anymore, then shame on you. Shame.

"So then. If I go rabid and erase the words, you'd still find some stupid way to continue your 'medicine show' for just the money, right? No matter how trivial or trite it would then be, you'd just push on mister greedy. That is if The Keepers even allowed you to continue such pointless floundering out here in the desert."

"But just look around us Eli. This is our only life raft in an insanely huge ocean of land. Plus obliging those drawn to our performances is still getting our message out loud and clear. Maybe even to people who are positioned to spread it further than could we alone.

"So *Against The Black Chrome Sun,* as presented by we Players simply will and must keep on keeping on. Forever and a day. Unless it's somehow proven that things should be otherwise. Or until another Someday, whichever.

"And don't forget that Elise is a pretty nifty writer too. Or as a last resort I would even bull-fluff the lines alone until I got some cheap hired hack up to speed plinking out speeches at least as good as are yours.

"And as she did before, Sophia would certainly stay to oversee whatever remained of Wulfsgate even if Zackery and Sienna went back into the mountains again. So I'd be no worse off. In effect it'd be a win-win for me, so either step off or else take your very bestest shot Here and Now. If it's a rumble you want I'm ready to dance. You?"

"Well Michael, The Continuum clearly got it right in allowing the concept of 'fickle is as fickle does', or something to that effect. As it seems you've turned your back on words both good and true. But no I won't fight you, as I refuse to duel with an unarmed man.

"It seems neither of us has any longer got even the slightest idea what to do Here. Not to help ourselves, let alone to continue doing something meaningful for those who come to the shows night after night, needing and expecting. So we've reached the end of our mission, nearly as I can tell.

"Huh, I suppose it is possible to eat one's twin after all. And I guess The Keepers were wrong about us needing the entire thousand year lead time. As already there are dead words crusted all over the killing field. Sad, as I'll get to write you no more speeches to help fulfill The Grand Plan."

"Oh for the love of, come on Eli. Wait a second and just lemme me catch my breath. Look, we'll work this out. Let's just talk about it, whatta ya say? Perhaps I rashly misspoke out of turn. I mean, there's no back-turning here. It's still all about and only for promoting The Magic Of Love.

"And we're always up for showing The Wulfyre too. I just got stars in my eyes, see dude? Oh you know, because *ABCS* is doing pretty good now. And people are taking more than a just bit of notice.

"Yeah, that's it. Oh come on, another chance please? I'll be a good boy this time, I promise. Hey, throw me a bone here kiddo. Let's let sleeping dogs lie until we figure out what's what. Moving on, faking it all the way until we can do better. Because things could be a lot worse. I've done worse. Ha, we've done a lot worse. So, can't we dodge the bullet here and somehow keep Wulfsgate together?"

"Oh blast. Fine Michael. Fine, but only if we really do move on. Really, okay? I'm game, only what's next you freaking nutjob? Cause believe me, right now I ain't got squat. Well, except. Ha, you do have that really pretty mouth. The one I've always craved cramming into.

"With more and more of my best words, I mean. I could probably do that, if you'd let me. Sure I could. Oh I'd really love to just stuff you full. What you say, dear boy? You want some more of me?"

"Uhm look Eli. I mean I love you more than life and all that, but you're freaking me out a bit here. Oh what the hey, I'll go with it. Uh, you've got that beautiful mind, yeah. The one I've always lusted after getting it on with. Getting more and even more of those spectacular speeches from, that is.

"How's that? Look, give us the best of what you've got in that fabulous head and we'll wow them every single time out there."

"Michael Michael Michael, you've got to agree that some where some time we must have done some thing really bad to deserve each other this freaking much. And by the way, I love you more than life too.

"So then we'll just pull ourselves together huh? Again. Then while I shadow the cast, whispering great new lines in their ears on the fly without them even realizing it - you'll be free to do that crazy kind of voodoo that only you do so well, with my complete blessing."

"My crazy voodoo Eli? What a great phrase for later, about which I'll give you full credit of course. So from now on we agree everything's a 'you go we go, fifty fifty', to well past forever deal? All for glory of The Magic Of Love."

"Michael, *Against The Black-Chrome Sun* is already more than just good. In fact it's good good. But look, when these last rewrites are in it'll be exquisitely perfect. Because it'll be the whole truth too. Exactly what we do best, and exactly what they out there need now even more than ever to relearn how to love."

"But just promise me Eli? Never another page which says only blah-blah woof-woof? Because I promise that even if it says that, the folks out there will hear it from me exactly as you wrote it. Well almost, or sort of. What ever."

"Easy promise my Michael. As any lines like that would, as no cognate writer ever committed to parchment: suck-ith. And up with that I can not put. But hey, who knows? I may even write myself some incredible lines to speak on stage some night. Finally letting the entire company and the whole world see me for who and what I really am. Oh don't look like that. Far stranger things have happened, both in real life and the theatre."

"And they would get it, whatever it is Eli. Oh they would, they'll just eat it up. See if they don't. But wait bud. How can we let those who can't come here to Wulfsgate and see *Black-Chrome* live experience even a tiny little bit of The Magic Of Love which we've so very carefully crafted into it? How?"

"Settle you silly boy, as it's not All Fall Down. Cause we'll simply print and provide plenty of copies of our play's script, once it's done that is. So now shut up and drink your wine while marking in the changes on these pages. But just be as good as your promises, okay brother?"

Handing Michael his papers with a flourish and taking up his own wineglass again for a more-than wee sip, Eli tips it toward Michael once it is empty and only smiles his secret smile. The one they both love and loathe.

FOUNDING WULFSGATE

TRANSIT:
Fade up from black to a blank stage except for eight nondescript chairs in a loose array toward the front. Michael enters from upstage center and crosses to recline across some chairs. Eli slowly enters unseen behind him and leans against the wall on the left to observe, as suddenly Michael stands.

MICHAEL:
Again the recurrent dream. Curiously detached, I watch cruel barbs shredding the flesh of my palms as The Wire continues to slither relentlessly across them. Looking up, I follow the length of its strand flowing from the point of my torture to the horizon of vision where the thin black line disappears into Infinity.

Taking a somewhat tighter grasp in spite of the pain I slowly force a turn upon my own axis, bending the living wire across my back and onto my chest, where it continues to constrict just at the heart's level.

Quickly wrapping the free end of this barbed wire over itself to complete an inescapable loop and stepping unsteadily back to set the barbs even further into my flesh, I cause a momentary stop or at least a pause in the progression of its unspiraling from The Coil.

I startle somewhat more aware. And surge skyward, as if striving for a liquid darkness's surface. In which

I flail as though in utero. I thrust my face newly birthed, above the plane of always-rising inkiness. Desperately gasping at first breath.

Blood's blade-sharp tang of burned copper assaults my senses. As grayness commences contorting itself through cracks opened by the rift of a new sort of dawn breaking, to bleach the night from my long black-wash of respite.

Morbidly fascinated, I gape raptly as crimson rivulets stream along the outstretched fingers of my mangled left hand. My writing hand, coated in the viscousness flowing from within it and now parading before my face.

And reach contented terms with that the volume of my very life-essence splashed upon the tiles during untold years of lessons while within this tangled wire of Love's Magic, has aggregated a placid pool within which I languidly float.

TRANSIT:
He rather excitedly crosses toward the left as Eli moves behind him to sit on the right, now watching even more intently.

MICHAEL:
Now completely free of the bonds of my nightmare once more and singularly celebrating the thundering pulse of heartbeats within this grandly heaving, no longer restricted chest, as they whisper: They were. We are. All is. I see. I know. I will.

ELI:
(sotto voice) And only a thousand more swift years remaining until our time is ripe, twin brother.

MICHAEL:
I'll go and share with them. Oh, soft please fool for of course they've known all along that this replaying vision in my addled head simply heralds that it's come Someday. So let them be held by me only a bit. Lingering mere seconds before their required recession toward the background.

And there. The fleeting moment surrounding this new dawn. Surely having everything to do with the peculiar play of Light and Dark, as a black-chrome sun reveals itself for the first time to show what changes the next hour holds for us all. As well as that my millennium in particular rises.

Oh but not so simple a progression toward their Forever. Having done all of what they were allowed and allotted Here and Now, they must withdraw and retreat to another place. Liberating energy enough to reform in others I will need to draw into The Keepers use.

And as they will yet hear me speak, I needn't say I'm sad or feel guilty. Because we three clearly aren't done Here, and neither did I in the least-wise banish them into yonder mountains.

TRANSIT:
Eli stands and moves toward him, taking his usual

but this time round's as yet unrecognized position just behind Michael's left shoulder.

MICHAEL:
Yes the world will now go differently. But there can't be resistance on any of our parts. Assured Zackery and Sienna will return somewhere, sometime else checking to see it through, I can be almost gentle. Let them reside here in my heart always and forever please Continuum.

ELI:
(sotto voice) Come Someday, come.

TRANSIT:
Michael turns and exits upstage center as Eli slowly follows him off with a contented swagger to his steps. The lights dip to black for a three-count, then come back up. Zackery enters from downstage right and pauses, staring off to the left.

ZACKERY:
Good, Someday comes. And The Dark is done again, for now. Though it also brings the last few moments Here as we are before our voluntarily abdication. Perhaps mankind is ready to move forward now. Perhaps the hard lessons were learned this time. Perhaps.

So what to say to her that I haven't already? But perhaps I've said enough, or too much. Either way there is yet this I must speak, though she is well versed in how it goes. Might I find courage and voice enough to say as is expected:

How shall I go further in exhibiting hopeless devotion, or displaying reckless abandon? Already splayed upon my back, unprotectedly exposed to The Universe. With no will for defense and thoughtless of its requirement.

Go on dear Sienna and dig deeply there. To simply take what you will and all which is needed to fulfill the want. Even unto my life's very blood, smeared upon your fur as the brightest war paint.

That is the dire necessity to win yet another battle in which we have engaged The Darkness so long and well. Zackery's on board for that, as our stated goal while any where any time has ever been to offer even our eternity to enable the success of this stand.

TRANSIT:
He almost absently moves to and sits near the center, as if totally entranced in or by these thoughts.

ZACKERY:
I cannot help but stare curiously detached yet morbidly transfixed. At the rich crimson pool which is creeping relentlessly across the lush growth of our killing ground, from the raggedly gaping wound ripped into my underbelly. Allowing the required repast.

At the edge of my blurring vision, I find you concentratedly licking. Reverently observing once again the ancient instinctual ritual of taking the spirit as well as the sustenance of the sacrifice into ones self after a successful takedown and kill. Then you graciously momentarily avert your focus after sensing me watching.

As I struggle my trembling paw toward your heaving flank, you suddenly pull away. Blood-sated but not having slaked your guilt the least, though we agreed you must. Viciously shaking your head sling me in silken rivulets from between the whiskers of your gore-caked muzzle.

Arching on your haunches to point your nose skyward, deliver a joyously mournful grief sonata to the stars. Signaling The Continuum your confessional vow of having completed this cycle of the work we'd begun together.

Before I convinced you to once again relieve us of that awful burden inherent between canines and felines, by such loving consummation of our reliance on more than life to enable the return to Forever.

Into which as The Keepers Design dictates, by sheer force of nature you've learned and practiced long and well the last thousand short years, you quickly slip beside me yet once again.

And linking paws we'll walk together one last time. Softly as we leave them, softly as we lead them, toward The Knowledge. The Knowledge. The Knowledge.

TRANSIT:
He stands and moves left to stop behind the chairs, seeming to recover from day-dreaming. Then turns to stare upstage right, sensing Sienna has entered there. She looks downstage to make fleeting eye-contact with him, then pauses staring off to the left.

ZACKERY:
(sotto voice) She comes, my tiger-tiger burning bright.

SIENNA:
(sotto voice) So he is afoot this soon, my timeless wolf. Meaning it has arrived at last, Someday. The end of The Dark again. Time for Michael's ascendancy. But then also our time in this Now grows short.

So what to say to him that I haven't already? But perhaps I've said enough, or too much. Either way there is yet this I must speak, though he is well versed in how it goes. Might I find courage and voice enough to say as is expected:

Now to evermore we will sense the very air as it whispers briskly through our whiskers. Refracting playfully from darker reds to richer blues in its fanciful dance away from the shadows.

And we'll sort every subtle nuance swirling around

these grizzled muzzles. Preserved vestiges of the marvelous heat and magnificent cool spawned as we've traversed Here together.

As we stretched skyward to grasp the very stars themselves, which were alighted as we passed. Casting soft glow upon all future history, so lessons shown and taught by Our Love will be remembered and applied.

And drew down enough energy to make certain the intent of our paw prints stamped into very stone by The Gate, leaving little doubt our passing. I love and loathe that the best of us was spent as we trundled by, and won't return by this path soon again.

He has seen me so I'll cross to him willingly, one last time.

TRANSIT:
With a sharp intake of breath she turns and quickly crosses downstage. Where they meet at the center, kiss and hold each other in close embrace.

SIENNA:
So then my true love, today has to be Someday? You won't postpone it and let all linger a bit longer in The Dark? Not for we two, but so Michael and his others have more time to tarry in This Is?

ZACKERY:
You know that answer as well as do I dear. It is come Someday as ordained. We didn't create this

tide and therefore couldn't hold it or change it, even if we wanted or intended such. And Michael-Eli's thousand year ascendancy period has now begun. So it is no longer up to us. We must simply content ourselves with that we were and even now are being allowed to serve yet again as The Grand Design dictates.

SIENNA:
But darling wolfie surely. Only a day or two more wouldn't destroy the timing of The Keepers ongoing plan. So let's momentarily hold back The Light, while we take a well-earned draw of breath for ourselves.

TRANSIT:
He reluctantly breaks the tender hug, gently pushes her away to the left and stares at her blankly. She moves even more to the left and stares back his direction, but now as if she is profoundly sad and sorely concerned.

ZACKERY:
Hold tigress, as I won't hear such. Each and every second forever past or future are all vital parts of The Keepers Design. All including us serves Time and Function, as a new sort of dawn has already begun to break upon mankind. That's why it must be, will be that today is Someday.

SIENNA:
Oh, but is Michael ready Zackery? Ready for all which must come next? Did we do our work with him well enough? I mean, he knows of course that we will be

gone from Now and nothing Here will be the same? Knows we will no longer be allowed to lead or teach or guide him, or them?

He is prepared enough that when you and I release hold of this Here and Now, everything changes? Prepared to step into the next coming maelstrom and do what he must? Is he prepared to teach what he's learned? Zackery?

TRANSIT:
He almost timidly turns away from her to the right in silent answer as she moves around the chairs and despondently sits at the left.

SIENNA:
Oh please dog. Please say that Michael at least knew in advance about today being Someday? And that it's timing is because of us?

ZACKERY:
No, those things I cannot say dear. Michael-Eli's not ours to command or protect or instruct anymore. And Someday happens in spite of us, not because of. The Dark is, must be done. Today.

And you know The Plan's design was that Michael-Eli know nothing of the timing of this chain of events until this morning. But in this instant, this blink of the cosmic eye - he knows all as of the rising of yonder black-chrome sun.

Just as he knows too all which lies within him and

what waits before him. The Keepers Plan remember? To take The Light away from humankind so they will appreciate getting it back, by learning of Love again. That is why.

Sienna look at me kitten. And this is also why I'm so certain he is prepared. But even if he's not totally so, he still has Their thousand year grace period in which to learn what he may not yet already know, or know he knows.

As well as that Michael-Eli and his chosen ones will perceive that preparation time as having elapsed during only the next thirty days following this dawn of Someday, and not the actual period of years it will take.

TRANSIT:
Slapping her hands to her lap in exasperation after having hidden her face behind them in despair, she snaps her head around to glare at him angrily.

SIENNA:
Wolf. That's simply not good enough. Even the half-light of the black-chrome sun is not nearly enough.

TRANSIT:
He moves in front of the chairs, crosses to and kneels pleadingly at her feet. She looks off right over his head as he pauses to compose himself before speaking in a more hopeful and confident voice.

ZACKERY:
Kitten. The Keepers have not, can not, will not make mistakes in how They choose to assist mankind via Someday. Nor in how They use those chosen to serve, just as was done and will continue to be done with us.

This new light will be sufficient for humankind to see the direction in which they must go. Your colors are bright enough to aid in this process and they stand for a more hopeful future. Mankind can learn the rest from what Michael-Eli teaches, per The Design. So he is what matters now. Please try to acknowledge that, at least.

SIENNA:
Dear I will as I must, trust in your trust that all will be well with him and for him. For it's true The Keepers have never failed, either us or humankind.

But Zackery? Why do you still insist on adding that other old name of Eli to his, as you've always done? Instead of only the one of Michael by which the rest have known and called him?

ZACKERY:
It is a part and parcel of him, and as it ever has been. His Other. But silenced to let him learn. Silenced to make him think. Just as we will soon be silenced to force his continued growth. It's his birthright, bought and paid for by the eking out of blood onto the pages of untold volumes, age upon age.

Before he or we ever entered existence for our first of what are by now innumerable strolls around The Universe this Other was most often referred to as Eli. The educator. And it logically follows, as that eager young student displaced in both time and space, spit out from the vastness of yonder desert ten centuries ago quickly became our wisdomed teacher. Long before our meager lessons to him were even partially done.

Michael-Eli will be Fixer and Lead Guide to all mankind very soon in my stead. That Other, Eli, will awaken in him again. As they are conjoined twins born to serve as one. So the name is completely fitting and proper and ordained. And it's also a sign of my very deep respect. So does any of this put you even a bit more at ease dear Sienna?

TRANSIT:
She stands while making a show of smoothing her clothes and slowly offers him her hand, but as if not totally sure she should. He takes it and slowly stands, turning to look off right as if ill at ease himself.

SIENNA:
It will just have to be enough then, what you've said. And yes, I can almost better let go of Michael a little more willingly now. If only because he is also part archangel. Isn't that so Zackery? In full armor and ready to enter the battles which must be fought? At least here in my heart of hearts he is.

But darling answer me this one other lingering, if silly question. In another millennium having passed do you think anyone will remember us fondly and think well of what we've tried to get done Here and Now?

ZACKERY:
Angel or not, waits to be seen. But I think what you truly mean by asking that not-silly-at-all question dear is, will anyone blame us? And I celebrate and fear that the answer to both parts of it is yes they will.

Mankind did not like The Dark. Perhaps through hearing Michael-Eli's true words under this dim sun, they will learn enough to earn back full sight after yet another gale. Brought by another looming Someday. And you must remember that we are not quite finished Here either.

TRANSIT:
She shrugs off the intended calming effect of his response. Then moves left to behind the chairs and glides past him to the right as if lost in thought, before turning back once again while smiling coyly.

SIENNA:
Oh then now do come with me, sweet furry pup. And let us away. There are still a few new morning stars to be seen. The first in a very, very long time. So let us go out into their faint light before it's gone.

For we needn't see every minute detail from here

as Someday unfolds, do we? And so before we can't, let's take one last long rambling meander about this precious hill we've tended lovingly and diligently here in the desert. It will all look very different without those old walls I am quite sure. Oh, do come now. Be a good boy, please?

TRANSIT:
Then without waiting for a reply she turns and exits upstage left, almost like a giddy schoolgirl heading off to a picnic. He watches after her in wonder, then turns back and sits at the center as if to hold counsel with himself.

ZACKERY:
I do so love that one with emerald eyes. She knows I should remain here where I might better monitor the coming of this Someday. But she also senses I won't really care to witness the implementation of it here by myself.

And she also knows too that I have never been able to refuse her, anything. Now she awaits me out there. Someday will progress regardless, and our last symbolic act of release can be committed from anywhere, can it not?

Surely better wherever that may be with her than anywhere else without. So away. As it seems we've still a walk to walk, and a talk to yet talk as well. About perhaps only the simple dreams of just a dog and a cat. Out for a long, lingering last stroll together around Here.

TRANSIT:
He begins moving right as if to exit, but suddenly stops and spins on his heel to stare upstage center.

ZACKERY:
My darling Michael-Eli. Now it comes your turn, so stay true. Only do that which you've always only done and all will be well, as it's not All Fall Down. The moon and stars have shone over you until now, soon this black-chrome sun as well. With my last breath I release a fondest wish for you and those who will soon stand behind, beside and with you:

Enter life from Darkness, then exit into Light. Whatever happens in between is because of The Magic Of Love. Many pass by blindly, while others see all. The only difference is what you look for while you are Here.

You have this. Show them how to learn Love again. Make it count, for however long this light lasts. More and brighter is coming later, but Eli's got your back. Play on dear boy. Now, come Someday. Come.

TRANSIT:
He snaps right once again, looking off as if making a decision, then moves right around the chairs and almost runs off upstage left. The lights dip to black for a three-count, then come back up. Sophia and Elise enter from downstage right and cross center in front of the chairs, already in conversation.

SOPHIA:
Under laboring breath I chant the fearful refrain:
Must go and tell Master, but oh how to brave Our
Wolf?

A thousand years passed, far toward forgetfulness of
how in those days his heart was so mangled. Though
in true course of devoted service, her's as well
included. So much selfless sacrifice from them both
while helping many along their journeys. And all I
could do was silently scream.

Oh, it's been difficult being this me I am, mandated
to only watching after. But there are few complaints
as I'm certainly no dewy-eyed neophyte. Gladly
having done duty since before Zackery was even just
a still-wet-behind-the-ears pup.

Funny that few knew of me. Though Sienna has
privately told she suspected that before her time
some other one must've been there. Helping keep
him on The Path and out of The Clearing, when he
couldn't or wouldn't help himself. But those days
passed. And now my life comes down to being an
utter and miserable failure in what will most likely
prove my final term of responsibility to Them.

ELISE:
Madame alone had I responsibility last, as alone was
I sentinel the time in question. So surely alone am I
now the one suspect. Rest easy, you haven't any
part of owning this day's discovery of issues.

Though believing I'd checked how all faired then doesn't offer solace now, for certain The Gate wasn't breached during my last rounds, when all was secure though still in The Dark. And only a few quick years give or take either way shouldn't have upset the rest of Eternity.

SOPHIA:
But to find The Gate damaged this dawn, and with such dire consequence. Sad fact of the matter now is that for the first time since They blessed the final travelers and shut them out in that day, all is no longer secure Here.

But don't pity when I lament. For though it was you on duty it was under my post and I don't shirk responsibility. Oh, certain willful latitudes were most always encouraged of course. Freely if I must say so myself, and oh I must I must so say.

ELISE:
But you only went off to conduct required affairs within the blink of an eye. I think it not rash that a blink may be defined as a hundred years, give or take a few decades. And what was or wasn't done by us either may just no longer matter anyway. As see? The chrysalis of our issues is that just outside yonder broken stone walls in the desert lies what I believe in my heart to be this desecration's true root and source.

TRANSIT:
She moves in front of Sophia to the left, pointing

and staring offstage as if at what she is describing. But Sophia moves to the right, wringing her hands as if deep in concern.

ELISE:
What I've seen is that yet another itinerant minstrel troupe, if a solitary 'lay-expositor' who fancies himself also an 'actor' can be termed a troupe - Long's Wulfyre Traveling Show or such - years back settled out there on our killing grounds.

And he's been doing something out there on our sand a long time now. Mysterious doings too. So busy, with all manner of strangers coming and going throughout the early hours of each and every day. And later in the evenings? Whole crowds. Often as not, numerous caravans of them.

Why even as I speak, see Madame? There are a mature man and a woman determinedly riding in toward that which passes for the tent's compound on what appear to be a pair of matched white horses.

Why, someone should have looked hard and deep into that fine kettle of fish centuries ago. I'm surprised Master hasn't had the entire lot of them cleared out, as was often done in other times near as I remember.

SOPHIA:
Same old same old child, and frankly of little import to me at the moment. There are other larger problems which may or not be associated with The

Gate conundrum. For in through its broken seal suddenly rushed a literal tide of most deadly Greyness.

Dealing severe diminishment to our Sienna's colorful gardens, which had thrived even in The Dark. Those of every rainbow hue, planted there inside our walls. Lovingly, faithfully tended by that one with emerald eyes. And perhaps worst now the tide is receding, taking the flowers out into the desert fields.

Atop that were it not already enough and clearly the most troubling, is this dawn. The first in ages, though just as in the cycles I've seen before. But something is different about today's daybreak. For gazing east across the desert, as he and she will or already have done shows that something is much amiss now that The Dark has been pushed back.

With not a significant cloud in sight to give any cause, the good yellow sun seems dim. The good yellow sun seems gone badly wrong. The good yellow sun seems gray, almost as if it had become black chrome. And why is there only this strange half-light?

TRANSIT:
She turns and crosses left to join Elise, following her staring for an instant. Then they turn and cross back toward center, where Sophia faces Elise resolutely as if in newly-remembered determination.

SOPHIA:
So with you in tow I'll simply go and tell what's been found. Letting the chips fall as they might, even if that's raining down on us. But I'm known well as a wolf and a tiger may understand any human as to how I have always conducted myself and my duties. So perhaps They won't be too harsh in Their reaction and response to today's news.

This seems clearly to be our fault, and doubtless we must confess our complacency in the events. But in what fashion? How to say it, how to admit it, how to phrase it? As delicately as possible of course, as has always been done. Which is both my forte' and stock in trade.

ELISE:
Then surely it's not All Fall Down and we will turn out still pretty-much okay. Wait and see Madame. Why yes, every thing's going to be alright. And doubtless Master will make it all better, for he still only does that which he's always only done.

SOPHIA:
Well perhaps child. After all he is now as he forever has been The Fixer and Lead Guide to us all, whether he likes it or not. So then let us go to do and to say that which must be said and done.

TRANSIT:
She turns on her heels, crosses right behind the chairs and strides almost marching, to exit upstage left. Elise turns to stare after her and pauses,

waiting as if uncertain of being overheard before she speaks.

ELISE:
(sotto voice) Uh sure, we'll just come upon them thusly. Soon as Madame musters the courage to approach The Dog Himself on the thin ice of this new kind of day.

Under laboring breath, I chant the fearful refrain: Must go and tell Master, but oh how to brave Our Wolf? Indeed.

TRANSIT:
She moves around the chairs to the right and runs off upstage left to follow Sophia. The lights dip to black for a three-count, then come back up. Michael enters at the center upstage and pauses as Eli follows a distance behind and crosses by the chairs to casually lean against the right wall. Michael crosses down to the center as if deeply lost in contemplation.

MICHAEL:
What to do now? Or next? I am lost, alone, exhausted. Drifting at sea as if in a leaky lifeboat. And where is this Other I was repeatedly admonished to expect and rely upon? Still I guess this Now is better since The Continuum's jacks like those walls yonder tumbled Someday, so to speak.

Yet the blues and I only are left to cry on the face of the wind, while of course leaving plenty of room for other lunatics. As a darker scene shows under the new black-chrome sun, except for Sienna's colors flowing across the desert. How brilliant they were and are.

It seems that dreams, smoke and mirrors are what've been left by Them for me to use. Well, plus this seemingly relentless pursuit of useless perfection of mine. Which is found only while strolling through the noise, up here. These will have to be enough.

But it's like swimming upstream to the core of it all, only to discover so much more to do. Unimaginable that it's still slightly less than only a month since Someday. As now I'm always writing lines or speeches, and hopefully well enough to have the desired effect The Keepers expect.

Plus it's not just scripting for myself anymore, but for the other four in this new company. So there will probably never again be idle time on idle hands for me. And while any fire going out leaves some things cooler, my abilities must not run toward the ignorant. For ignorance is ignoring what is heard.

TRANSIT:
He moves distractedly to the left and sits despondently, hanging his head in despair. Eli crosses to sit on the right, watching Michael as if entertained.

MICHAEL:
And how might I ever do well enough? As I already

obsess over content and context, in abject terror that audiences will find us ridiculous rather than profound.

Though I was taught it's all outrageous if one is doing it right and trusts the proof in The Magic Of Love. Cold comfort now though. Still, oceans can only be experienced one drop at a time, loving and loathing. And boats always leak most exactly when needed.

But now is the greater need for surviving and helping them to somehow do the same, as time grows so short in this Here. Oh how do I juggle these myriad marbles while also keeping them all in only one basket? To my great sorrow try as I might, I cannot see any clear way to make this possible. So perhaps it is now at last come time to let All Fall Down.

TRANSIT:
He pauses, then lurches to his feet and staggers toward the center, putting his hands to his temples. Eli holds his ground, as if drawing Michael to him. He moves even closer to Eli, seeing him for the first time. Eli stands and only stares back as if perhaps smugly amused.

MICHAEL:
So what the deuce is this then? Hold, oh hold Here. For the love of all that's Love, hold most dear head. What then? Some thing. Some one. Some Other, suddenly here within me. But get out. By my bones and fur, get out.

ELI:
Oh settle you foolish thing, it is only me. Nothing new to discover here but your own heightened awareness, as I've always been just over your left shoulder. But until now you weren't quite ready to know me. Weren't quite ready to see me, to feel me, or to touch me.

MICHAEL:
Other? Eli? Oh, it is you then, Eli. Reawakened here in me just as was repeatedly said you would some day be. But barely before show time once again is cutting it a bit too close, don't you think? But so then Eli. We'll write for the members of this close company, the best that we may.

Only please. Might we somehow avoid coming across as scenes out of some campy old wild west medicine show? I want no leftovers from when I did that very kind of thing during The Traveling Show times out in the desert. Knowing no differently, so not being able to do better.

ELI:
Oh, it surely will be enough to make a difference. But only if we do well enough together. This new Wulfsgate was intended. Ordained by The Keepers as a stop-gap ripple here at this crossroads of the world between dawn and dark of night.

And only as you are able to deal with that none but you will know I am the voice within, less they think you mad or madder. If so they'll come to believe you've simply gotten that much more experienced at scripting. I say this only for the art which lurks within Love.

MICHAEL:
(sotto voice) Okay, but here's the thing. Now that you're back we better press pause so to speak, rewind a bit and take care of some business. I sense nothing but a considerable confusion out there. So maybe you better gimme a little help with what're the proper lines to say in order to bring everybody back up to the same speed once again.

ELI:
Hold simpleton. Regardless what you think you learned at Zackery's and Sienna's feet, you haven't right or wisdom to conjure or recreate yet. What The Continuum is, it is. I am to be known to you and Zackery only for now, and not by the rest of The Company. You cannot be a Geppetto fashioning me from The Unreal in your own image to suit your limited vision. They will not allow it, nor will I. But come, let me cogitate some. Then we'll confer a bit.

TRANSIT:
They both cross to and sit center, then converse in many soft whispers a protracted length of time. Michael then stands and slowly moves to the right while staring at Eli, who nods repeatedly. He then addresses the house almost confidently as Eli watches closely to see how Michael handles this difficult assignment.

MICHAEL:
Imagine a million lifetimes. Then several hundred more mortal generations in quick progression. And let that to current understanding be but a blink of the cosmic eye along this unseen highway we're traveling, you and we. Or us and them if that offers you more ease. Rambling and meandering under the familiar glow of the good yellow sun.

An okay thing, as long as the important questions remain the same. Though mostly without resolutions along the way. Allowing for maintaining your grand illusion that during whatever time you're granted in this Here, some will work out many of the necessary answers. By which you will be greatly comforted, as you'll believe those people and ideas lend guidance in learning your required lessons.

Though most of those will probably remain modern mysteries. But what if some random dawn any morning remaining, Someday let's call it - Someday you awaken into a radically different world. Either gone quite mad, or come completely around, dependent on your perspective.

TRANSIT:
He pauses as Eli stands, crosses to and whispers into his ear again a few seconds, while Michael repeatedly nods as if in agreement.

MICHAEL:
We bring this up because, apparently that exact thing has happened recently or is happening now.

See? No? Then we'll lay it out for you in somewhat more detail. Separating The Light from The Dark, so to speak.

Someday is in process of breaking dawn right now, far as you know out there. But on our side of the lights it's already been quite a long while. A paradox which is a guarded secret, but one which Eli says it's okay to tell.

The Keepers and we carefully planned this so you didn't have to sit through a thousand years of boring expository scenes, while we worked out details of exactly what must be in our upcoming play *Against The Black-Chrome Sun,* on opening night. In other words, we've done what's needed to move the action along. A little clever folding of The Continuum so to speak.

TRANSIT:
He looks at Eli for his approval, who shakes his head negatively and takes a couple of steps left. Angrily turning to face Michael, pointing and pausing to regain composure before dramatically making an impatient flip of his hand.

ELI:
(sotto voice) You're welcome Michael. But The Continuum and Keepers be damned, that was all me. And you best not forget it, if you expect me to carry you. But yes, stagecraft at ones' fingertips is a marvelous thing. And now everybody's back on the same page again?

Good, because that's all the time and effort I'll put into explanations. So be a good boy and finish this up.

TRANSIT:
Michael visibly cowers at this dismissal and turns back to face the house as Eli wanders left to lean against the wall. Michael moves further right and pauses staring at him, who ignores it.

MICHAEL:
I guess we uh, now return you to regular programming, joined already in progress.

So while Light and Dark once again argue over which actually owns this one particular hour, you will notice a pretty significant difference as this Someday dawns. That being the absence of a yellow sun. Oh but hold, for there's nothing new to fear.

Not if you can see that the calming down trick simply involves defining just what changes brought by the coming of Someday might actually entail. And how they may have various impacts down on your individual levels. For there is still a sun, though now black-chrome hued.

This is also when you must learn to begin seeing the world differently. For without doubt, amazing new times have now been thrust upon us. So mustn't you seize opportunity to make this a time of Knowing? Knowing how to give more and better Love, thereby being more and better loved in return.

And of knowing this could be your final full measure Here in which to draw a last breath intended only for some other.

Color has won over The Grey yet again, allowing you and your significants a wee bit more time to try getting this Loving thing right. And perhaps to even earn a bit more 'regular' light a little further on down the long and winding road. But that still remains to be seen, pun intended.

TRANSIT:
He pauses yet again looking at Eli almost pleadingly, and now openly unsure of himself. Eli simply shrugs and crosses to beside him, pointedly speaking only to him before moving on to sit at the right front of the stage.

ELI:
Perhaps you might do well to refer them back to that concept of illusion you sort of mentioned earlier. As it just may serve to abate their discomfiture or rather their shear terror, further along during Black-Chrome.

MICHAEL:
True, and dear friends if you can do as he says, we're going to have such lovely experiences the next little while, you and us. That's a promise.

TRANSIT:
He turns to and moves toward Eli, who joins him.

Both somewhat reluctantly extend their hands in a half-hearted shake, while Michael speaks only to him.

MICHAEL:
So let's play on sir. And we'll see how they like us then.

TRANSIT:
They turn left around the chairs and exit upstage center, still intently discussing matters in whispers. The lights dip to black for a three-count, then come back up. Zackery, Sophia, Sienna and Elise enter downstage right actively in conversation, crossing up midstage to sit randomly.

ZACKERY:
Well Sophia, for Sienna and me almost everything is different since the dawn of that Someday leading to this half-light which is shining on mankind for now. And yet in its own peculiar way at the same time nothing changed.

SIENNA:
And how amazing that my myriad colors are not only everywhere now, but so dazzlingly brilliant, despite this new dimness. Oh how mankind deserved a break from The Greyness of so long.

ZACKERY:
Then one morning we simply rode in on horseback to Michael-Eli's old show tent down in the desert. Which marked our return back into this brave new world of the black-chrome sun from our self-imposed exile.

It's what Elise told you before of seeing, Sophia. And regardless of a few lingering memory lapses which are more of a nuisance than a problem, we are Here to serve. As still, we always only do that which we've always only done.

Mostly it seems we've been with all of you forever and a day. Part and parcel of this company and of this place appropriately renamed Wulfsgate. Apt, since we each had to pass through our own figurative gates to arrive Here.

SOPHIA:
And so it seems to us all. And we've almost convinced ourselves that is the entirety of the truth. Of course Zackery, you know Elise and I didn't ever get the opportunity to brave you Our Wolf, for telling about the unfolding events of that now long-ago Someday.

TRANSIT:
Elise looks either guiltily or conspiratorially at Sophia, then quickly turns to speak directly to Zackery as he stands and moves around the row of chairs to stop behind the one in which Sienna sits.

ELISE:
Well there really was no need at that point was there? As you already knew all events and had interacted with them accordingly. Why you had even already left the building so to speak, you Sly Old Dog. And taken beautiful Sienna with you, or uhm something like that.

SOPHIA:
Nor did any from that Then, including Michael far as I know, ever experience your physical presence again before you returned innumerable years later. Though in many ways it feels like only yesterday that we were walking and talking with you both on The Hill.

SIENNA:
Oh how much I get that. Time passes differently Now than it seemed in that When. Why I remember those two lovely white geldings we were riding as if it was earlier today, not hundreds of years gone.

TRANSIT:
She stands, crossing to the left lost in remembering and turns back to look at Zackery. He looks after her in return, as if seriously pained by knowing how she feels about those events. Elise stands and crosses to join her.

ZACKERY:
Of course we now understand it was all only to allow for more intensely detailed consideration on our parts. For yet while it was a mere eye-blink to us, a thousand years passed for mankind as they began to perhaps relearn how to use Love again.

SIENNA:
Part of me still misses our time away, my wolf. And we each could have chosen at any point along this winding way to simply sit this turn out. Merely by

invoking the unexercised options we each had always owned.

ELISE:
And of course granted acceptance of the responsibilities each also had for deciding in favor or not of learning and teaching new tricks. Just as The Keepers expected we would each somehow figure out.

ZACKERY:
Thereby helping humankind make some sense of today's Here and Now. And to see how to proceed given enough sight, in which cause we are now submersed. Playing out Michael-Eli's words to the innumerable folks who come each evening expecting there to be, Something More.

SOPHIA:
To which effort we willingly and repeatedly give our all, as if seeding the ground. Allowing this company's accumulated words and works to scatter on the wind, dispersing down to the millionth part.

TRANSIT:
She stands and crosses to the right, staring offstage.

SOPHIA:
And in the dark of night just prior to Someday's dawn the compound's walls tumbled down, literally and figuratively releasing new Light and life into the world. I still miss its security, though now I would have it no other way.

ELISE:
As only then could our next unrehearsed dance set begin, both off and on stage. Remember how those first steps we took in both places resulted in not only dropped lines, but a few face plants too? We were all learning so many roles at once, about theatre and about life.

TRANSIT:
All four begin to move from their places at almost the same time, crossing to join at the center as if being drawn together.

SIENNA:
But rising gracelessly on newly-penned lines and unsteady confidences we shouldered assignments. Just in time to stand, deliver speeches and turn to face the music. By which actions we railed against becoming redundant fools on this repurposed hill.

ZACKERY:
And for a brief time those retained states of old left-over Knowledge served to mask the horrified grown children cowering within, which we really were in that Then.

SIENNA:
Understandable as well, I mean after all we were preparing to entice mankind to dive into free-fall from sanity's cliff.

ELISE:
But only so they could have face-to-face

experiences with either learning to fly, or else with accepting the perpetual fall from Grace.

ZACKERY:
Which is the truest way to exchange Love, when all is said and done. Exactly as was hoped they'd figure out. Now nightly shared through such awesome words. Oh, those lovely words.

TRANSIT:
They once again turn in unison and cross to sit, but each in a different chair than before. Then Sophia abruptly stands and crosses to the left as if extremely agitated.

SOPHIA:
So it was all to let those colors of Sienna's flow out into the darkened world wasn't it? For inside the walls was the repository, a warehouse, waiting as the world changed toward this new way of seeing. Toward this new way of being. Toward this new way of Love. Though some, resisted - and still do.

TRANSIT:
She pauses as if realizing she may have lost control of her emotions. Sienna looks at Elise and they stand, crossing to join her as if to offer reassurance.

SIENNA:
But we got to announce to the world for The Keepers that the black-chrome sun was expected by The Grand Design and that it initiated Michael's move

toward his legacy. Toward him, leading them back into The Light.

ZACKERY:
It seems we were ordained to band together in pursuing what was called for by that cause. Dedicated to growing this theatre and its other varied art forms.

ELISE:
Helping Michael continue the mission for which he was born and groomed. Along the way learning that if there is nothing worth giving a guffaw to in the script, not to dominate the laugh-track onstage.

TRANSIT:
They all turn to give her very odd looks and then sit once again.

SIENNA:
None could have figured this facility would ever help so many so much. But Zackery did, my stealthy wolf. Just lying in wait for the ripening of time to release the storehouse of resources to multiply and disperse.

SOPHIA:
And now on this revered hill is another gate, literally and figuratively in place of the long-ago broken one. Here it's stood for eons, sturdy as its first day. Intended to represent a new testament to opening up and letting in or out, whatsoever comes our meandering way.

ELISE:
Fittingly we assimilated into this troupe from Wulfyre
Traveling Show, perfecting its stagecraft out there in
the desert so very long ago. To become not only
tribe, but family. So we may present meaningful
shows nightly, just as Michael was doing decades
before this most recent Someday.

TRANSIT:
Sienna slowly stands and moves left before turning
to face the others.

SIENNA:
I still catch that Far Away look in Michael's eyes,
when he thinks he's alone or he doesn't realize I'm
watching. Which scares me more than a little.
Though perhaps his wandering through The
Continuum is finally done.

TRANSIT:
Zackery and Elise stand and cross to hover beside
her during the awkward silence which followed. Then
Sophia stands and makes a show of consulting her
watch and adjusting her clothes, purposefully
breaking the mood.

SOPHIA:
So say we one, so say we all. But this moment think
me an ogre well as company manager. Oh don't. I'm
old not deaf, so I hear the talk behind my back. Now
each of you. Go rehearse, putting in the lines and
pages written or re-written for tonight. And you best

be quick about it too, else you'll see the sole of my boot as it comes your way.

TRANSIT:
Zackery, Sienna and Elise almost laugh but then think better of it and hurriedly exit offstage to the right instead. Sophia turns to watch them go, wringing her hands as she faces back to the house.

SOPHIA:
If only I was comfortable erasing that line between us. Especially with Zackery. Such a dear, as are they all. If only to let each one know even a bit of how much they're honored and respected. But I dare not trust that The Magic Of Love is real, else in that openness they would think me only a weak, daft old biddy. Or perhaps not. Huh'mm, I will ponder this a while more.

TRANSIT:
She slowly exits to the right in contemplation. The lights dip to black for a three-count, then come back up. Elise enters from upstage left looking around uneasily. She crosses in front of the chairs and creeps down to the front center, conspiratorially waving shyly to the first rows of the house.

ELISE:
(sotto voice) Hey. Hey, come over you guys. But ssshhh. I'm supposed to be inside doing a bunch of pre-show stage and house stuff for tonight, but telling stories to you out here seems an eversomuch more delightful way to pass late afternoon.

Like about the many who've come to Wulfsgate over the years since He and She originally departed. Or of placing a foot into one of the paw prints stamped into the stone by The Gate, while on some pilgrimage. And of hearing the hallowed-ness whispered about the amazing works from innumerable artists hanging on only thin air in The Galleries.

But I myself think it's for the beauty in the colors of innumerable blooms spreading all directions into the desert far as one's eye looks, which speaks so loudly within each chest.

For that represents what They knew and what we now know our world would, could or should become through the power inherent in giving and receiving better Love. Just as we Players try to show. As that may be all which mankind truly needs to ensure survival.

Hey, now this is cool. A simple bronze plaque, hand-etched, adorns the massive ironwood gate which now stands open to Nowhere, Anywhere and Everywhere. I can quote what it says from memory:

TRANSIT:
She almost floats to the right and pauses, striking a most heroic comic pose while getting totally caught up in the moment.

ELISE:
"Caressed by your naked hand I merge into your

very essences. With no guarding barrier between, as we're stripped of all pretense or persona down to the last revealed truth. Connecting my fiber to your synapse, with damage to flesh or bone or wood not withstanding. Though yes it tends a bit messy as your flow streaming pure red stains my wavering grain.

So then cleanse as you must, to enable a firmer grip on the brushes which paint The Universe. And wiping that crimson on your robes so when done, you might hang those garments on the nearest hook. Becoming intentional masterpieces on the showcase wall titled Love.

Though you ask, must we retool again yet so soon? As surely it's been only a few centuries since the last tearing of ourselves open, when you were my rest cushion as I was yours. But indeed we must.

Wine glasses are at hand, though one must lift one's head to sip. And in that perspective of looking up at the works we've concluded, inspiration comes to continue creating from within that placid pool of us. Thus adding to this prized collection."

TRANSIT:
She crosses left and sits as if to better compose herself as Sophia enters unseen from the right and pauses, watching her intently.

ELISE:
Oh, don't fail to notice 'Not For Sacrifice At Any

Cost' signs posted near every work in The Galleries. You see in Wulfsgate all serves Time And Function as a stop-gap ripple at this crossroad of the world, between break of dawn and dark of night.

SOPHIA:
(sotto voice) So my protégé and presumptive successor has learned her lessons well indeed. Meaning my faith in Elise's abilities was not misplaced, as she does fine. A bit more tempering and she can assume her rightful place.

ELISE:
I always thought The Wolf meant that the choices of no walls being rebuilt and Wulfsgate permanently standing ajar send a clear message that open-ness is best to illustrate mankind's evolving or devolving passages.

Or maybe, not remembering if one just came into some place or group, or if one is preparing to go out from them or there are both equally good. Anyway, such cool words The Old Dog wrote.

SOPHIA:
(sotto voice) You speak true for one so young and tender, Elise. But like mine for this still nearly-new child, no contentment lasts forever. As there is always something lurking out There, demanding further attention.

TRANSIT:
She strides over to stop beside Elise. Who jumps

up and almost falls as she stumbles backward in surprise at being discovered, as if she was a bad girl caught doing a questionable deed.

SOPHIA:
You there Elise. There's more important work you need to be about. So close your yap now and get yourself back into the theatre. Last check to the front of house. Call fifteen minutes for the cast. Then cue the first lights.

I swear there are days when I believe my manager title means that I can barely manage not to cuff your ears. Get now.

TRANSIT:
Elise exits left hurriedly, looking back over her shoulder. Sophia watches after her, before turning to face the house as she moves to the center. She looks off left again as if making sure Elise cannot hear.

SOPHIA:
Apologies dear people. She's kept you tarrying too long out here with her silly stories and the like. For though it's only a short walk from here to the seating, there are important decisions to be made among yourselves before getting to finally sit.

Terribly important things like the choice of wine or ale or even forbid, water. And if one needs a pre-show pee or not of course. As your total pleasure and complete contentment are my major duties now as ever.

But. Might I have a moment? I've a tidbit here in my head that I seldom have or take the time to speak about, and therefore most don't know. So shall I tell a tale? Fine.

A while back a dog-eared scrap of parchment was found under a smooth white stone on The Hill nearby during my daily ramble and meander. The dating of it is unknown and some of the hand-written scrawl beyond legibility, but we Players agree on who penned it.

It said in part: "... that the walls have gone is no big deal, except it left us homeless. But leaving those old lives behind will solve that. The Keepers' Grand Design is served. And humankind gets to linger Here a while longer.

New gate stands in a stone surround, on-duty sentry in silhouette beneath the half-light. Hand-hewn and weathered just long enough to still contain the life of naked wood. Worn glass-smooth from pawings as we've passed to check the ramblings and meanderings, as to how their progress goes."

Indeed, such great words The Old Dog wrote Elise. Oh now. Look who's forgotten herself, by his bones and fur. For holding you up or back even longer, my pardon.

But there are other shows scheduled should you rather defer deliberations until later, simply choosing to wander the grounds and galleries more. It's not All

Fall Down, as Elise could easily exchange your seat-chits.

So dears go in or stay out as you will. Though your decision either way should be very soon. As you'll have only exactly enough time to settle in or not, before the next staging of The Wulfyre starts.

TRANSIT:
She turns left and pauses while consulting her watch to cover her apparent discomfiture, as if suddenly embarrassed and confused by this newly-found openness with total strangers.

SOPHIA:
Now with your pardon I go about my business and leave you to yours as well. Fairest evening.

(sotto voice) What the deuce was all this then? Oh, indeed there must be strange influences of some sort in the air tonight. That wasn't like me at all, bother it.

TRANSIT:
She suddenly and hurriedly exits off left. The lights dip to black for a three-count, then come back up. Sienna enters from the right upstage and regally crosses downstage left to sit, though uneasily.

SIENNA:
Oh, it breaks my heart that in dear Michael's weary head, this morning like every dawn a mob storms this citadel. To tear him down from the false peak

and cast him far along the slippery slope. Crumpling cowardly to the desert valley's floor.

Where he fantasizes they dance on what's figured his carelessly abandoned corpse. About which he believes the critics are smugly convinced, except for a single stubborn flicker. Too confidently ignorant of their cruelty to even begin to accept that the show's viability isn't spent or kaput.

Not that those slights aren't real and felt to him or that such spurning doesn't burn him deeply. For I know he silently screams yes to both. But which results in only more and better lines.

To the point that with him being an avowed dramatist, each and every sham death takes a toll. Culminating in the sort of literary blisters which spew forth amazing words, and by which the performances we give grow in complexity.

And by such toils he daily claws the torturously winding way back up to ground level. Nor do the detractors ultimately matter a mite. As those wonderful words of his have indeed gotten scattered on the winds down to that millionth part.

(sotto voice) It pains me so, but such is how his life goes. Oh sweet loving boy, play on my darling.

TRANSIT:
She stands, smoothing her clothes. Then glides off to the right. The lights dip to black for a three-count,

then come back up. Zackery enters from upstage right and crosses down to the left. He glances up at the center before turning to the house and pausing.

ZACKERY:
My typical late night behavior. Still post-show hyped, I've stepped outside to take the air. Perhaps also sensing that just over The Hill, rest does not come easy either. If at all.

ABCS staged by we Players has been running for decades now. With pages and lines having been written, rehearsed, re-written and re-rehearsed again and again and again. And oh it's good I dare say. Very, very good.

Seems there should be little work on it left to be done. Surely isn't everything in proper order for the fade up from black tomorrow evening? Time for the well-earned black-wash of respite? So one would think.

TRANSIT:
He moves right, as if lost in thought. Michael and Eli enter upstage center, cross to in front of the chairs and freeze standing back to back.

ZACKERY:
But as I peer a bit deeper into The Darkness further away, yes there. Two tiny ember-glows at the tips of some of those stinky, twisted little cheroots they have become so fond of smoking along with that strong, nasty-looking dark-red wine they swill.

The dog-clown twins lurk down there upon a darkened, empty, crumbling stage. But not engaged in funny business now. As where the old show tent is in process of gracefully slow-motion falling, still unknown to all The Players but me, Michael and Eli have literally separated into two, only to walk the boards together.

Where they ponder if how they and we present and represent The Wulfyre can be better. If it could or should be somehow, more. Brooding on their perceived past failures and arguing about their proposed future challenges.

TRANSIT:
Scuffling his feet almost like poorly-done, badly-practiced dance steps he turns to stare upstage center in profile.

ZACKERY:
Pushing little pieces of stuff around the old platform with his boots, Michael paces as Eli not-so-gently lends his input. Both stirring the cast-offs as though remembering that it's the sweeping up which is vital. And afraid they may have missed some bits as they went.

TRANSIT:
Looking out toward the buttes Zackery pauses, as if seeing again in his head just at the desert's dark horizon two other once-unidentifiable silhouettes against the moonglow.

ZACKERY:
Both of us were with a shovel in hand, turning out rancid earth one patient scoop at a time. But to what end, do you suppose? Perhaps putting The Past to uneasy rest by digging deeper with each effort. But only just deep enough.

For other than would shut out what must always be experienced, some lingering contact being necessity. For how else to know? Oh she and I, we two understood the labors of our time. As so shouldn't you all.

At least in order to speak truth when one says that they know Love. That is enough. It must be, for it's all we've been allocated with which to work. But it's honest as well. Interesting how The Continuum always works those minute details out so cleverly.

Listening intently, I hear them muttering between themselves as they are known to do occasionally. Odd bits and pieces of forgotten conversations neither can quite wrap cognate memories around. Perhaps even an object lesson and prime example or two we showed.

Not-so-internal arguments as to how or why something should be rewritten again. Rather expertly simply doing as was learned: that every canine must worry a worthwhile bone enough to get out the best marrow.

TRANSIT:

Zackery turns back to face the house, exaggerating the motion for effect and moves toward the center while glancing upstage over his shoulder again.

ZACKERY:

I turn almost contentedly, knowing they are only doing that which they've always only done. Working The Craft, by crafting The Work. Dealing with their own demons in velvet.

But by my bones and fur. A splash of good scotch, some draws on a fine cigar and then darling Sienna's warm bed are now calling out strongly to me. So I go, as I must.

(sotto voice) Play on Michael and Eli. We've all got your backs.

TRANSIT:

As Michael and Eli cross to the right and pause, Zackery exits at the front left. They move toward the center and turn to face each other.

And, this is about where Against The Black-Chrome Sun truly starts give or take a few more lines. It is also almost exactly where we first came into this little dustup many many speeches ago, if you remember. So it seems as good a place as any for us to take leave of this or that Here and Now for the moment, don't you think?

There is a quick fade down to black.

BY THESE STRIPES

My boon companion and I as was our custom on innumerable dark and bitter winter's nights sat imbibing while ruminating philosophically and taking notes regarding the same. Drawn up to that black fireplace in the street-level side room at Ye Olde Cheshire Cheese where the likes of Dickens, Doyle, Tennyson, Twain and even Wilde had sat in times before.

When rather abruptly, to the staccato accompaniment of sleet once again relentlessly pelting the leaded window lattice, Zackery plunked down his now wineless glass, and turning to face me simply and boldly said, with a theatrical toss of his head and a flourish of his hand:

"So dear friend. There's still another story of my youthful days which you've never heard me give voice to during our many years. But if you're game then so am I, feeling compelled through camaraderie and/or inebriation. And therefore am properly liberated or lubricated enough tonight to finally unburden myself of it out loud. So what say you to that, good sir? Shall I share and tell a tale?"

More than a bit perplexed but equally intrigued, believing we had priorly shared the entirety of our past personal stories, and also somewhat taken aback by this unusual openness to take a break from our spirited discourses of more theoretical topics, pouring liberally for us both, I merely nodded my eager willingness to attend him faithfully. And so at that he began:

"Quite late one foggy but fine spring evening many years ago, I unexpectedly found myself on what I thought at the time was to be simply another of my mental journeys through the magic. How and why this event occurred at that particular time I couldn't then, and surely can't any better now, say for sure. Perhaps I dasn't know.

"But none the less, as there sat I with my glass in hand, half-dozing over a treasured old volume of Doow's poems in front of the well-banked and hardly-smoldering fireplace, suddenly a road just opened up before me.

"Now dear sir, you need to understand that in this particular case unlike in some other similar yarns which I've shared with you, it literally and physically started less than seven feet away. Right in the very room where I was lounging, piercing completely through the solid masonry wall and away out of sight into the surrounding night-time countryside.

"Well needless to say I was very most intrigued, and felt compelled, nay even obligated, to follow to conclusion wheresoever it led. So excitedly putting aside my wine and book, pulling on my boots and taking up my coat, hat and favorite blackthorn, I did just exactly that. Out I went, though cautiously, not willy-nilly. Where said pathway meandered aimlessly hither and yon through gently rolling, heavily wooded vistas. Between overgrown thickets and beneath massive first-growth trees surrounded by lush groundcover. Until both it and I eventually came to a crosswise intersection with yet another road, at almost right angles to the one upon which I had most recently been traveling.

"Now, this newly discovered pikeway I immediately deemed to be of some greater import than the surrounding country lanes, since it was much more graded - wider and seemed somehow grander than the one I had been following. And it was topped, dressed or paved with what appeared a crushed stone mélange of a sort I did not recognize as commonly being employed in the local pastoral infrastructure.

"Then most suddenly, as I had stepped directly onto the center of where the crossing point lay, I unimaginably beheld a rather large - no extremely huge, nay fantastically gigantic feline. Being of course more precisely a tiger. But I can tell you here and now sir that a most unusual tiger she was, even with her enormous size notwithstanding.

"I venture the pronoun 'She' to be used here, because even though I perceived nothing overtly that would in the leastwise indicate or convey any sense of maleness or femaleness, it nonetheless seemed to broadcast being undoubtedly a female of the species. But perhaps this soon I digress about the gender rather needlessly."

Zackery took a pause here as I expertly refilled both our cups to their brims, with nary a drip wasted upon the polished table top. Pouring from the pitcher perennially perched near at hand, which the bar-backs never let run to dry or toward empty. And taking another long, contemplative pull of the preferred vine rouge while peering at me steadfastly over the goblet's rim, he spoke once again:

"For the most remarkably striking aspect of her appearance was far and away her unnaturally-hued coat of fur, as it was all quite red. And I mean to say sir, the boldest, brightest shade of crimson imaginable.

"The very colour one thinks of whenever someone says that something was blood red, for it was all that and more. And its condition. Its condition was exceedingly strange as well, in that around the edges and fringes her pelt was remarkably torn raggedly, bedraggled and scarred.

"The thought came immediately to mind that in this condition she most closely resembled a horrifically battle-scarred warrior after some long, arduous and abysmal combat. And as well sir, completely gone were any tinges or vestiges of the normal or usual orange, black and white shadings which one would associate with this type of animal.

"One other profoundly disturbing thing is that I got the distinct impression that she was angry. And oh no, not just angry, she was livid. In a total internal rage. And once again, although there clearly was no outwardly visible sign to telepathically or otherwise communicate this emotion, the unmistakable idea was readily apparent.

"It almost seemed as though her state of mind actually rolled off her like unto waves in the ocean. Each and every succeeding one exponentially stronger than the previous, and each increasing in its ferocity. Needless to say I was absolutely terrified by this visage.

"Dearheart I'm not at all ashamed to admit that while you know me to be no coward, in this particular instance I dropped my old hiking cane, turned tail and simply ran like a spooked pup. I wish to Great Hound that I had owned the courage to at least stand my ground somewhat longer or better. But alas.

"And suddenly, at once I found myself most totally lost, alone and very thoroughly disoriented. For though my whole young life I had stalked these forests, and indeed thought I knew this copse of woods like the back of my own hand, I no longer perceived any clear way at all in which to move.

"Infuriatingly, the more twists, turns and switchbacks I made in trying to unravel my lostness the more confused and discombobulated I became. Apparently plunging blindly deeper and deeper into the tangle, instead of in any way bettering my lot.

"At very least though I had thankfully escaped the terrible vision with which I had been presented scant moments earlier. And having so acknowledged and finally feeling safely secure for the time being, I attempted to compose myself if only for vanity's sake.

"But then my friend, directly in front of me from still deeper into the tangled thicket came the same tiger out to meet me again. Now this clearly was entirely impossible, for she would have had to flank well ahead of me at remarkable speed to have accomplished this feat. Yet, there she defiantly was just waiting for me to turn about."

Then Zackery paused again, seemingly staring intently into thin air at absolutely nothing while absently pulling out a wrinkled silken pocket handkerchief with which he slowly wiped the left side his face. Inside my head was only the recurring refrain of: Tell me more Whitewulf, tell me more. Then daubing at his red-stained lips after having taken a veritable gulp from his glass he paused yet again, before following with:

"Oh yes. Most undoubtedly one and the same as before. But now she appeared miraculously well and whole and remarkably healthy. Totally unmarked in both her coat and flesh. Though neither her recovery nor her appearance there in front of me now was even remotely feasible, she had in some manner accomplished both feats simultaneously.

"And the most unnerving aspect of this whole series of improbable events was that she now just stood stock-still there, only watching me with those incredibly vivacious but unblinking eyes. Which I instinctively knew could alternately either melt away the coldest icicles deep within ones soul, or else freeze them even more solidly.

"Then with but the merest flick of her ears, she began to regally glide towards me. Mearde, I was literally riveted to the very spot upon which I stood, visibly trembling. As the longest time imaginable seemed to spin out in front of me, she closed relentlessly nearer and nearer to my indefensible self.

"Expecting, yet fearing with utmost certainty the worst to come from our second and most probably our last-ever meeting here in the midst of these woods, having no defense I made a vain attempt at bracing myself. As surely coming next was a terribly crippling death-blow delivered by one of those gargantuan paws.

"Or perhaps worse, a lingeringly lethal bite by those massive jaws somewhere upon my unarmed self. Agonizingly allowing me to know my life was slipping away in a bright red flow. And only now remembering that in blind panic I had earlier abandoned my trusted shillelagh, after a vain warding-off gesture I closed and covered my eyes in preparation for impending disaster.

"Then I merely waited with acceptance for her to strike me dead, for there was little else to do but anticipate the inevitable. Most astoundingly though none was forthcoming, as timidly peeking between my splayed fingers showed the giant tigress simply passing by on my left, apparently intending to only serenely stride some few paces further down the lane.

"But then she turned as we passed within two scant feet of the other, as did I. And so in that clearing of the woodlands, in a dazzling patch of unobstructed sunshine, we locked each other's eyes for the first time.

"Hers were green. Green, green. The greenest of greens. Greener than Ireland. A green I'd never seen before or ever since. An almost unimaginable green. Green enough to put mere emerald gemstones to shame. Green enough to make even time itself stand stock-still in dazed amazement of that green-ness.

"Still reeling from this visual onslaught while fighting hard at partially recovering myself, and from what I now judged to be a rather safer distance I then inquired - somehow intuitively realizing that she would understand language - as to her immediate intent of me.

"And in truth sir, yes there was already much more than simply idle curiosity involved here if you must know. An interminably long pause, until then she spoke all or rather most of her incredible life story in one seemingly tremendous rush of unburdening herself."

Here Zackery pointedly held out his cup to me for its replenishment, as it had gone quite empty and therefore was wanting. He canted his head a bit, as if listening to ice pellets of yet another brutal London storm pummel the glass as I enthusiastically complied to his unspoken request, pouring into mine also as he slowly refocused and continued:

"So according to her splendid narrative, she had once been just a regular tigress, as she so succinctly phrased it. As if such a creature ever existed. And indeed she had even spent most of her life up to that point experiencing nothing at all unusual, and being more than a bit disappointed in that regard.

"Then following some ill-disguised, or at the very least ill-explained or perhaps purposefully glossed-over turning point or change-evoking events in her mostly mundane life, everything had just quite suddenly changed.

"According to her claims, it was really nothing more complex than her simply realizing exactly what and who she actually was, which had caused her to somehow become as I saw her now.

"She said perhaps a literal swelling with the pride she wore, had grown her into the monstrous image presented to the world. Pride in being fiercely independent, in being totally aloof and in being self-sufficient. And of being remarkably able to take full responsibility for retreating into her cave of shelter for preservation, any time she needed or wanted.

"But I also thought I heard some hints of great anguish at her being forced to do the same at other seemingly inopportune times. But she seemed completely mystified as to exactly how feeling that way had actually caused the incredible morphing through which she'd lived to tell me the tale.

"However it seemed that she clearly understood and accepted that choosing to be as she was now seen by the world condemned her to a life somewhat in solitary, and of a continuous if often apparently wanton wandering by herself alone throughout the world at large.

"Me? I simply stood there staring, dumbfounded into being mute. Transfixed and totally enthralled by her tragic yet touching story, and not knowing exactly how to or where to or even when to begin responding. And certainly not knowing in the very least what the proper words to offer might be.

"Then what I should have in retrospect anticipated, but what at that point was the last thing I would have ever thought possible, actually happened. She unprovokedly attacked, as suddenly a massive blow to the side of my head knocked me sprawling to the ground, reeling and almost senseless.

"Stunned and on the verge of losing consciousness,

I fought somewhat vainly not to black out completely. Thrashing blindly and wildly out at whoever had assaulted me. But I could see through my panic only the tigress, looming."

At this point, Zackery raised his goblet to our eyes' level. Swirling it rhythmically so as to better admire the great beauty of the legs the rich ruby nectar it contained made. Then laying back his head, he tossed it down in one smooth swallow, vigorously draining it dry. I refreshed it as he recommenced solemnly:

"Even in my very addled, near to delirious state, a part of me simply refused to even consider the possibility that it was she who could and would have attacked me with such brutal viciousness. And indeed her loud weeping, wailing and other protestations of concern as she rushed immediately to my aid, seemed to clearly bear out that idea.

"She oh-so softly cradled me to herself, much as any cat would do for an injured kitten, while stanching the steady trickle of blood from my newly split and aching scalp as best she could. Through which actions it seemed readily apparent that she must have been only my true savior, and certainly not my violent assailant.

"Although at my hesitant questioning she was overly flustered and at a tremendous loss to explain who my attacker was, if not she herself. But as she continued holding me steady, cooing, no purring to me very softly that everything was fine and that I would soon be okay.

"I too began to dismiss her as a possibility. And then inexplicably it happened, almost like a sorcerer's spell descending upon me. As I suddenly began to see with a full-blown clarity and understanding the depth of feeling the tigress held inside herself. Good Dog do help me, I began to want to somehow give those same type feelings back to her as they welled up from deep within me.

"Too late to be helped by the deities or The Universal Continuum or what else have you, and with a slowly dawning horror, I realized that she and I had begun falling in some version of love, infatuation or whatever else one might say passed as those emotions.

"To my all-too agonized astonishment, and in one great rush the events in which we'd become so utterly and hopelessly, helplessly involved became clear as crystal for me. But such emotional disasters shouldn't ever happen to any mortal human, and just couldn't in reality be happening here and now.

"It would so completely ludicrous, a tigress and a man immersed together in an inter-personal relationship. Oh no sir it wasn't at all natural or rational or logical or ethical for certain. And it wasn't least-wise proper by any and all known accepted standards of gentlemanly behavior.

"And last but certainly not least, it wasn't even remotely what I wanted or needed. But apparently she did, the sly hellion. And she was just so damnably persuasive in her insistence of it, without even saying so. In that she was somewhat coy and rather cloying, both at the self-same time. But mostly? Well having no other way to phrase it, she was seductive beyond all logical reasoning.

"And as ridiculously cliché as I know this must sound to one of your enlightened background, in that moment I seemed totally powerless to help myself. Overpowered and enraptured and defenseless, truly I was lost sir. Far bush-whacked off the beaten path toward the abyss, and scared witless of the prospects in the self-same moment."

Once again brandishing the woefully empty cup, Zackery paused as if in rapt contemplation of the myriad frost crystals on the panes separating us from the melee of weather out there as I for another of innumerable times refilled not only his wine, but mine as well. We raised and tipped them toward each other as he picked up where he had last stopped:

"Well before there was time for even a flash of recognition or contemplation, let alone fleeting understanding or acceptance, she had totally enwrapped me in what seemed at the time many more than only just two legs. And began to pull me relentlessly closer and ever closer to her striped self.

"Then oh Great Hound her mouth, or rather muzzle, was on my mouth and seemingly everywhere else on my face and head at once. We kissed if one could call it that, and kissed again and again and again. Though for me it was a bit more like being mauled. For hours it seemed it went on and on, all lips and whiskers and fangs and fur.

"But perhaps friend just perhaps, I do now truly believe by that point I had well and truly already abandoned the very last shreds of reason, or maybe even lost what passed for sanity itself to the throes of that unorthodox embroilment often basely referred to as animal passion, or lust.

"Probably and even hopefully both in that one instant was the only explanation. But at any rate, that this whole sordid and sad series of events could or should have happened only in my feeble mind, even now with time having passed I will not and can not accept. For it was all too grotesquely, gloriously real to have been simply imagined.

"But, inexplicably soon I was starting to feel remarkably better about my part or role in the entire experience and almost surely trusting my sanity again. And so far as to her the tigress, whenever I chanced a glance in her direction she just smiled her very special secretive smile. And smiled and smiled, until I wanted to simply become completely unraveled.

"Until finally realizing, I had somehow found myself professing first affection, then alas devotion and finally even love most true. I was both ecstatic and horrified. But all these in vain and to her apparent scorn, judging by her display of demeanor. For saying the least my dear, she was anything but bemused by our recent antics. I was however totally bewildered and befuddled.

"So like an errant schoolboy caught in a minor deviant act, I further expounded upon the life-long fascination which I had with tigers in general. Soundly seated on my throne of delusion that this action could or would of course help explain something, anything, or maybe nothing at all. But bound and determined to go down valiantly trying at any cost whatsoever.

"Here my dear boy lies the inception of love-loath. When was I crazy or just amazingly stupid she demanded to know in that next moment. And what did I expect from her or of our meeting anyway, as if I had rights to expect anything. Then as suddenly as begun, she stopped her tirade in mid-sentence and just laughed right in my face. Yes, love-loath was in full bloom.

"Turning profile and resuming where she had paused, she simply claimed to be yet again something I hadn't seen. Only this tidbit of insight was offered me and nothing more. Oh, then casually adding that she was not at all really a tigress, and or ever had been. More like an onion is how it was stated.

"Finally, was I totally deluded or addled or perhaps in some state worse she inquired, and I should stop as I was scaring her badly. Oh yes she indeed had said me scaring her. Me, just this one wussie poet, holding within himself no defensive devices but a remanufactured heart and an unsharpened pen, somehow scaring her. Really."

Here Zackery quite suddenly reared back in his chair, staring toward the textured-plaster ceiling far above. Dramatically dropping his depleted glass into his lap and putting both hands to his face. As it rolled away I reached to retrieve it from the rug, expertly filled it almost without thinking and returned it skillfully to the table. Hearing the blade-sharp clink of glass on the wood, Zackery stared at it a moment, picked it up and spoke again:

"But how was any of this role reversal even remotely possible? With too many questions to answer, it had yet not occurred to me to even begin asking them of her. But after some extended time of having totally retreated into what soon became a terrible and looming silence, she finally spoke in sotto voice that I was invited into her nearby private den to discuss the matter a bit further. If I should care to so do.

"And oh yes of course I very readily agreed. For egad man, I would have followed her literally off the edge of the world or anywhere upon it at this point. Of course already knowing all of this to be the case, she only turned her back on me glancing over her remarkable shoulder while simply smiling that secret smile yet once again. And so without further ado, off we went.

"But therein lay the rub, to borrow a phrase sir. As I simply couldn't help but begin to notice that in the brighter light into which we passed while emerging from the dense woods, she was indeed already beginning to look somehow and somewhat different to my eyes than she had in just the prior moments before.

"Now I'll beg you to bear with me my dear friend, for utterly and bizarrely ludicrous I know this next part will sound to you, as it certainly also will to my own ears even as I will be recounting it. But I'm duty-bound to tell it to you in all its full gory detail, as I simply must for your sake of complete understanding. As you will soon come to recognize, comprehending the meaning of the story deserves and even demands it.

"Then and only then perhaps, might you and I share some insights, post-tale. So altogether too soon we arrived at her dwelling place, her den. Alright sir, as it begs the saying, I will say yes even of iniquity. There, are you satisfied?

"Most of the visual details of which are much too sketchy to stick in my shaky mind's eye, and therefore now I no longer remember most of the particular particulars. But I do still see all too very clearly, burned into my retinas forever the enduring image of this phantasmagorical creature silhouetted against not one, not two, but three sets of sturdy wrought-iron bars.

"Which then unceremoniously slammed into the earth behind us, thus barring the way from her cave back into the reality of the world. Then quite suddenly my dear, so much so that even the best naked eye could not begin to follow the change, the tigress was totally and completely gone.

"Utterly transformed, remarkably replaced and truly transfigured into the most fantastically glorious woman I had been privileged to see, in this or any other of my several remembered lifetimes. She had inexplicably become the most incredible creature of the female persuasion one could conceive to encounter in any location or scenario imaginable.

"To simply say that I was struck dumbfounded would not even begin to express the sensation, indeed would be laughable as an attempt of adequate description. And Good Dog do help me, as damningly worse in that instant I was totally stricken by an overpowering consuming desire and need. As unbelievably unreasonable as this seems, and as profoundly disturbing as this was to my singular disposition, beyond physicality even the necessary chemistry was there."

Zackery paused in putting the wine vessel to his slightly quivering lips, turning it downside up. Thereby signaling it was once again in need of fill. I sat mine recklessly down to take his, which I only then realized had for some time been dangling emptily from my own hand. I tilted in and sloshed a goodly portion of the deep red pressings into each. And after taking it up again he almost whispered, post sip:

"Everything one could ever imagine was suddenly in place to commence a relationship, including an imaginary mutually-shared history. Even as the rational mind railed and screamed that fantasy never can or will live up to reality. During this drawn out moment in time, in actuality only the merest instant, she had never said a single solitary word and had never stretched a marvelous muscle. But then good sir, perhaps before we either even realized the implications of our actions, I swept her swiftly into my arms.

"And oh yes, she came quite willingly enough. Much more than willingly enough it seemed. We tumbled down onto the soft ground. A tangled mass of legs and arms and faces and torsos and nails and hair, all wrapped up in want.

"We lay on the cutting edge of lust, gasping on the crumpled leaf-carpet, behind those tripled iron bars. Most of my rumpled or destroyed clothing and all of our inhibitions in equal proportions each, having by then flown in all directions. And then literally casting our fates to the winds, oh Great Hound, we joined again and again and yet again. Never seeming to have gotten enough.

"Until we both had our fill and were once more fully sated. As we had drunk most deeply from that loving cup which seemed to have been denied us both for too damnably long. At once both found and lost completely in trying to cleanse ourselves within a rich pyre of glorious purification. Then we dozed, or else passed into some other detached state of being.

"I startled aware some undetermined time later. Totally and tragically spent, and terribly disoriented about the nature of it all. Alone and oh so very naked in every conceivable fashion, inside a cave I remembered not in the least. But with the painfully intact impression that the joyous event of that long murky night was obviously forever over and completed.

"Even so physically and mentally used up as it seemed that I was however, morbid curiosity still got the better of me, as I raised my head off the ground. And then I just simply stopped the movement as abruptly as I had started, for I caught first-sight of my hand as the field of vision swept across the area in which I lay. Something was amiss here.

"In fact things were much more than a wee bit out of kilter or off center. Oh by The Dog, everything was wrong and wronger here indeed. But not about her, as she was still nearby. Casually standing most beauteously just a short way off leaning against the tripled bars at the cave's entrance. Very much naked, and just as nakedly staring at me, while patiently awaiting my return to consciousness.

"As much as I then wished with every fiber of my being to still be asleep and dreaming, I knew I was most definitely awake and too much alert. Because I could see and all too clearly take in the true nature of the situation. And therein lay the problem with my hand, or at hand.

"But I just simply would not, or rather could not force my intellect to process the information that my senses were taking in. Or perhaps I was choosing not to make sense of it. Perhaps for fear of crossing over into that state of insanity from which I could never return or escape."

Stopping and raising the cup, Zackery drained it and licked his lips dry. Then dramatically proffered it to me, while turning to admire the now unrelenting snowstorm outside our window. Knowing my role or part in this now-nasty business well, I obediently poured yet again into each and as he partially refocused, handed his back. After drinking off much of it, he began anew:

"But then more's the sorrow, every little thing which I had been holding at bay and arm's length regarding the sensory-wise input of my eyes racked itself into place. Oh how I wish to Great Hound that it had not actually done so. But, I do pride myself however on the tremendous power of will I exerted over the course of the next few seconds.

"And if I was to judge by the incredibly shocked and utterly amazed expression now on my oh-so recent paramour's face, my actions, reaction or lack thereof must have truly surprised her just as much as they did me.

"For you see my distinguished comrade, I did not utter a scream or even let loose so much as a whimper. So just why do I digress into describing a seemingly trite act of reason and about an equally seemingly effortless act of only self-control, you may be asking yourself? And it's a valid question my dear. To which the answer is elementary.

"I slowly and calmly looked around once again, taking in the rather complex entirety of my station and situation. And then composing myself rather expertly, simply said in her general direction that by both The Good and Great Dogs it would seem that I myself had during that night become the tiger, instead of her.

"A profoundly understated act of pure mind over body control indeed, as by now you surely have come to understand. And by the time that ridiculously ludicrous statement had left my now thin black leathery lips, we both understood that I had merely stated the obvious with complete and total comprehension. Then utter calm descended and peacefulness settled itself upon me all at once, like some well-loved lap blanket as you may like it or not.

"And I can strongly assure you that while I most certainly did not so like, the simplest fact of the matter was that I was now a ferocious feline, no longer a human man. Yes my friend, I was indeed the ultimate cat of the species, which she just as clearly no longer was. Same horrific size she had been, in this case even edging toward the grotesque. Same silkily-furred coat and muzzle she once had. And the same four somewhat shorter stoutly muscular striped appendages which hers had been, just as any tiger.

"I remarked to her on how most remarkable it all was, and how very cleverly magical she must truly be to have engineered this amazing and even miraculous switching of places with me. Trying to sound casual, and ending my compliments with: so Brava and well done and now take it back.

"No response forthcoming but her deadly silence and an even darker stare, which stretched out a seeming eternity. During which time I came to both the realization and acceptance that most probably I would be spending the rest of my time on this mortal plane a tiger, not as the pretty-much devil may care, wine swilling poet cum philosophizer I always thought myself to be."

At this placing his once again dry goblet much too carefully upon the table Zackery unsteadily stood, reeling like a novice sailor who hadn't yet gained sea-legs and staggered away. Apparently in pursuit of the necessary. I paused, then slowly refilled our glasses with the vital essence yet once more.

Much time passed. Drawing out from seconds into minutes as I pondered his possible though not probable non-return - just as he lurched back into his chair, reached for his wine and said softly:

"By now to me even in my shocked state this seemed almost perfectly logical. As she'd somehow mysteriously traded places with me, thereby freeing herself back into the world of womanhood. And probably not doing so with magic for the first time I would be most willing to wager, judging by the oh-so smug self-satisfied countenance upon her exquisite features.

"Trying yet again to convince her to revert this result I knew would certainly bear no new fruit, as there was still no answer or comment whatsoever from her on my previous polite request. But it did cause her to one last lingering time slowly turn to and cast an even brighter more dazzling smile my direction.

"Though at that point she only did so to rather curtly thank me for the magic I had helped her produce and apply so liberally. And that was apparently that and the very last which she intended saying to me.

"After this she only continued to smile the secretive smile, whether to me or just to herself I never would be allowed to know. During this slowly pawing through and donning some of my still-wearable clothes. Which she rather more than expertly extracted from the tangled mess we had made of them.

"Reinforcing my impression that this was not her first time around that particular park, so to speak. As for me myself and I, knowing we no longer had need of them, we simply lounged there in the middle of the cave and slowly licked our left front paw.

"Now my good man, I know a bit about the many uses of magic in its multiple guises of love. In fact immodestly I could say I know considerably much more than just a little of those concepts. And yes even now as always, in writing there would be small letters beginning each of those words.

"Up to that point I'd never even bothered or believed in the sorts of magic or love that capitalizing some letters for effect purported. That concept I still prefer until this day to leave to the likes of Elliott and Wood and a few other of the poets I consider august.

"But no matter that now. I do completely believe though, that during the midst of our most heavenly unions, she and I had apparently made between us more and different kinds of the magic of love that night than just the kind you find simpered about over the books of erotica many hold dear.

"Then quite abruptly, either The Universe or I

blinked yet once again and she was gone, forever. It was all done so it seemed, and I was once again left only to my own devices. An island of one. And I was most definitely a tiger.

"Which was not at all in my mind when on that simplest evening I had walked adventurously through the damned study's wall. Just intending the indulgence of a modest and moderate stroll to see where the cursed path went.

"But as I lingered and lolled deep in that den attempting something approaching composure before action, my mind was repeatedly drawn back to the subject of magic again and again. For that if anything might yet be my salve and savior and grace. Allowing me to extract myself from this most uh, inconvenient situation."

Zackery finished the vessel's content at one huge draft, stared at it somewhat disdainfully and rather more forcibly than required thrust it toward me for its innumerable servicing. He looked hard first at me then even harder back at the cup when I did not instantaneously fetch the decanter for refilling it this time. Still holding it out toward me like a stubborn adolescent while merely sighing and staring me directly in the eye, again he spoke:

"Mon ami I fear that I mis-spoke before, though why I dasn't know. But most readily and freely I now admit that going forward from those events I acknowledge both versions, magic and Magic or love and Love all together.

"It had dawned on me that yet once and again oh just perhaps, perhaps All was not irretrievably Fall Down. My former station may yet still be attainable. But intense study and research were going to be needed. Simply those and nothing more. So I there decided and my direction was crystalline clear.

"First to love me as I was, and then to pursue the magical path. But I must candidly tell you in brutal honesty, that what with me stopping to admire the reflection of my fascinating new self in every little puddle or farmland pond I happened across, it took a blessedly interminably long time for me to return the distance to my home over those rambling and meandering pathways.

"Though obviously I finally and safely got back to the blessed sanctity and secure sanity of my most humble abode. And oh yes, just as I had surmised along the winding way, when I arrived there was absolutely no sure-sign whatsoever that there had ever been a rift, hole or portal of any sort anywhere in the wall of my lounge.

"Now. Suffice it to say that some great measure of time then passed, but I neither can nor care to know exactly how much. As I had committed to the formidable task at hand and therefore secluded myself in the library for the duration. I supped when absolutely required and smoked cigars like a fiend.

And of course quaffed huge draughts of red wine hourly. But only to keep my internal resources reinforced, as you have no doubt done yourself.

"Relentlessly in pursuit, I continuously poured over and mined into the ancient tomes and other remarkable manuscripts I was most fortunate to have secured in my possession over the years. For the answers most simply had to be lurking in them somewhere. Why my dear, even histories of entire lost civilizations had been meticulously written down and thus laid open to my eyes in those assembled works.

"So I was not overly concerned that the proper working formulae were recorded somewhere therein, awaiting only the finding. And oh yes of course, I eventually did find the final and resolute answers. Though for most certain perhaps not each and every single one for which I may have been originally searching. But mayhap so many more for which I didn't even realize in that moment that I had been seeking my entire life.

"And as is so very often the case in extenuating circumstances, I did not even know the full extent of the questions which needed answering. So how then could I not be even more than ultimately satisfied with whatever knowledge I gained? But it is safe to say however that everything has worked out exactly as it should, or could.

"Then again most things surely often do. If we mere

mortals can manage to let them stew in their own juices for a long enough gestation period. Do they most always not? As they simply always must. Oh yes as they simply do. Even so, I believe you would ask at this point: How have I fared from that then up to this now?"

Almost fearfully or painfully or pleadingly Zackery stared again at the as yet still empty glass, then back at me. And in a fit of absolute remorse in withholding the necessary libation from us both, I poured for a truly innumerable time yet once more. I offered him the vessel, which he gleefully took in both hands as if it were The Holy Grail itself. And as we shared a knowing nod he close-to slurped from it, then said:

"Oh Gad. You foolish individual and aiding abettor of those who are cherished old friends and of unknown new ones as well. For voila´! I sit before you here in The Cheese do I not? Ha! And how do you see that I be? Am I not a solid man among men? Appearing whole and complete and whatever else would cause concern for my well-being. I, Zackery Crighton Whitewulf say well to all!

"No most dear sir, there are no felines, not here tonight. No tigers here this evening I tell you, none at all. Ha and ha! So now don't be impertinent while I finish this story up for you, as of course I have learned many new and exciting things to share. Guaranteed to be far more than just the paltry answers I needed at the time to satisfactorily resolve the immediate problems concerning my future.

"But thank you anyway my good man for your oh-so loving care and concern in asking after the most obvious! That being: Doesn't anyone seeking his or her truth tend to always finally arrive at that point where we have hopefully learned? Hopefully at the end-point where fresh ideas abound. Hhhmmm?

"Uhm-er, speaking of fresh. The analogy of lovely cream rising to the top of a bowl comes to mind for some strongly exhilarating reason. And I do so like both churned butter and the soft cheeses you know. And rare-cooked meats from most any animal will do rather nicely. Oh yes! But only if almost raw. And poultry or seafood sautéed in duck fat with a wine glaze?

"Well that is close to cat-nip for people, most certainly! Now do pardon my prattle, but I'm not really sure just how to remember if. Hhhmmm. Particularly if I have always liked those things and most especially when together. Oh yum! Yes-in–deedy, it seems I've developed a very many new likings over the course of these last few short years. But oh well I guess that's of no matter as ones tastes surely change continuously. Oh indeedy-do, things do change!

"Ha! Anyway, anywhere and anywho eventually I think yes, there must be some shred of a moral to this little telling. At the least I suppose you would expect one would you not? As your kind of incipient inquirer seems to be particularly fond of that sort of a resolution thing. Do you not, for is it not so? Well is it or isn't it?

"But, Good William liked to tie up his little plays and such into the tidy package did he not, so why would I not as well? Ha! But alas my very most best of boons, I dasn't know with what to end or how to get to there. Nothing much comes to mind in terms of a wrap of sorts except for maybe this: In this case it seems the ultimate reversal was true.

"Ironically, curiosity created the cat, and 'twas satisfaction which took it away! Oh ha! Oh Gad man, do write that one down for later to be sure, as it was awfully good, it was. And there you know all that I know of it. Well that and perhaps this little bit of a ditty, stuck in my head almost since then:

'Oh you've got to kiss a tigress or two boyoes - as you pass life by - oh that one sweet time - you've just got to kiss a tigress or two - tah-dah!'.

"Oh goody! And so mon cher, here's done and done. For that's my story. Or rather a tale really, or call it a mere trifle. Ha-ha! But as to is it the whole and entire truth of the matter? Think as you will, but I'm not telling more as I've told you quite enough for one evening's sitting. And you are of course at free-will to believe how you must. So just ha on your collar, sir!"

I slid the wine decanter smoothly across the table toward him as he saluted me with his once-again empty goblet. Then Zackery looked away quickly as if indicating that I had been forgotten in the instant. And so I attempted to stand, resultant in quite unsteadily plopping right back into the chair.

But he snapped his head back to stare at me again, as if with the eye of a raptor now seeing directly into my very soul. Then speaking almost as he were a miraculously new man, or certainly as if a very much-more unburdened and therefore clear-headed one, he succinctly said:

"Now be gone with you as I simply will not indulge your every whim, and blast it you simply must be able to decide some things for yourself. But as for me, myself and I, well of course we believe nay we know, that everything I've shared you here on this very eve happened most exactly as has been related. And little more's important than believability.

"Oh, where is she now and how do I feel about it all you would ask as a double-barreled parting shot? Okay then, as you will. I'm quite certainly sure she's still nearby somewhere. For instance here in my head. Here in my heart as well. Good Dog knows she had and yet has those both until well after the end of Eternity.

"To blame or culpability then? Neither. She and I just both happened to visit the very same cool-water well at the very same moment, is all. None was coerced against their will as all eyes were wide open, with each getting only what was so ardently wanted or desperately needed. Perhaps even what was earned and therefore richly deserved. And it really could have been no other way, now could it? Should it? At least I would not have it be another way.

"Now go bother yourself sir. Goodnight and fare you well you sweetest of the sweet you. And I'll expect to see you right here at this self-same table again on the morrow's damned eve. You hear? Oh I am so much in need of plenty more of that bad but good red red wine."

I took a required death-grip of the table's rim and rose to my feet, repeatedly swaying more than a bit. Trying to compose myself enough for passing out onto the iciness of Fleet Street without incident. Vanity shrieking in my compromised head that I simply must somehow manage to vacate my beloved Cheshire with some shred of dignity still intact.

And ever-so reverently, as to no further cause disturbance, what with him still so highly agitated from the emotions of the telling - I turned to Zackery intending to convey some last small parting comfort, just as he leaned toward the table reaching for the wine vessel yet again.

Zackery's long, untied and by now most unruly white hair had tumbled off of his shoulder. And on my bones, The Good Dog's pelt and The Great Hound's graces, I'll forever swear that there was a small irregularly-shaped patch of short striped orange, black and white fur on the back of his neck.

I blinked hard and looked again, but he had swept his hair somewhat back into place. Almost as if he might've sensed that I'd already seen enough, or perhaps very much too much. So I gathered up my accoutrement, turned on my heel without calamity and slipped out the door into the frozen pre-dawn darkness of London Town.

But ask again that which I didn't quite hear please. Oh. You dare ask that of me? Must you have my opinion? Truth then. Zackery Crighton Whitewulf to this very day speaks only that, come what consequence may, even unto his occasional detriment. So I must not will not cannot doubt his veracity.

And knowing full-well that truth is often the pejorative of understanding, I must nonetheless take the stand that each word he uttered on the subject at hand was bonafide, by virtue of having been written into perpetuity by my own unsteady yet unfaltering hand.

But say. Are you not yourselves reasoning human beings? And have you truly not comprehended all by this point still? Oh surely you will not disappoint. As I would expect that you've at least commenced to begin to start to piece together this charmingly clever ruse petite of mine, Oui?

For yes dearies, part and parcel with each the same are we, Zackery and I. Inextricably intertwined. As two halves of the same heart we were, are and always shall be just the one cursed beat. Us. Whitewulf until well after the end of forever's last blinking. And so, thanking you each I'll gleefully take great eternal delight in having deluded at least me if not some or all of you, thus far into this story-thing.

For the adventurous exploit which I penned all by myself, swilling glorious wine in solitary that salubrious winter night in order to make the memories even a bit more palatable, transpired almost just exactly a bit in somewhat the way I have told it - this time. Believe it or not and like or not, here you have it.

There is no more comfort, cold or otherwise, for you to be had of me here tonight, as I am so done with both it and you.

For now.

AGAINST THE BLACK-CHROME SUN: ACT ONE

TRANSIT:
A slow fade up from black to a blank stage. Except for six tall stools or armless chairs in two sets of three with a space between, forming an arc at the center. One each lower chair with arms is set at the front of the stage both left and right.

Elise enters from the left back of the stage and crosses to exaggeratedly adjust all the chairs. Slightly moving each and putting it back in the exact same place, ending with the one at the front right. She pauses looking left over her shoulder, concern on her face and in her demeanor.

ELISE:
(sotto voice) Okay Sophia, all here in the house is ready for us to play once again. Though something doesn't feel right at all. Funny how Someday not only changed our daily palette, but seems to be coloring everything after. Young I was when you called me, saying it was for my defining of heart matters.

Was it so I may some how help mortals love life Here a little better and longer, or am I supposed to take away something for myself too? Either or both, it's not All Fall Down. Though I fear we shall soon see if you chose well.

TRANSIT:
She pauses yet again, as if still trying to focus on exactly what is troubling her so, then hurriedly exits

off right. Eli enters at the center back of the stage and crosses down front to sit in the chair on the left.

Zackery, Sienna, Sophia and Elise enter left also at the stage's back, greet and hug each other and move to sit randomly in the row of chairs. Michael enters at the center of the back of the stage, crosses to and stops in front of the now-occupied chairs.

All freeze as a recorded voice-over announces:

"AND SO THE UNIVERSE BLINKED YET ONCE AGAIN, AS THAT LUMBERING BEAST STILL LIMPED RELENTLESSLY ALONG. THEN PERHAPS THE LAST SURVIVING GUN ER-AH WORD SLINGER, SEEMED TO SIMPLY APPEAR. HAVING BEEN SUMMARILY SPIT OUT FROM THE SPACE TIME CONTINUUM. SURELY A THOUSAND YEARS AND MORE AFTER THE LATEST AND GREATEST IN THE SEEMINGLY ENDLESS SERIES OF NUCLEAR HOLOCAUSTS FOULED THE BELEAGUERED EARTH. BUT YET, HE STILL ONLY DOES THAT WHICH HE'S ALWAYS ONLY DONE. SO HE COMES UPON US THUSLY."

TRANSIT:
Michael moves down to the stage's front center as Eli stands and nervously crosses behind him to sit at the front right. Michael turns to and nods at him then faces back to the audience in the house.

MICHAEL:
On the thin ice of yet another day's end, welcome friends. To this little dust-up, welcome. To a night

quite rare. To a night unlike any in what passes for your hum-drum lives. Welcome here, welcome in. Oh yes in most certainly.

All you saints and sinners seeking a way to bring on some Light. All you lower or higher leavings of the brightest or the dimmest. Plus all you in-between souls who've come around close, yearning to hear and know the truth. Though that in itself surely is anything but self-evident or easy.

I am your best cousin, who would never lead you astray or deal you unnecessary ill. Professing that you each were ah, invited here this evening not for entertainment only. But to increase your enlightenment.

Me, who while being this Michael Long rode on The Whitewulf's back to rail against the deadly Darkness. And so to perhaps only dance with, not on you a bit. Twirling us in the pale moonlight while casting down my meager pearls of wisdom as if before the learn-ed swine. And we'll see how you like us then.

TRANSIT:
He moves more toward the right looking intently at Eli before facing front again, now seeming somewhat and somehow a bit less sure of himself than before.

MICHAEL:
Michael. Who familiars have more than once confused with Eli, as was often called us by some.

But let's not head down that road as none of us should really know.

For we, this small company of mis-fit toys and I, up close and personal Here and Now are The Wulfsgate Players. And we are about to bring you Wulfyre.

Now we will attempt to restrain and constrain ourselves to only what my writing alter-ego has composed into our book. So as to be most certain of getting the words out and directly into your waiting ears just exactly right.

To have the desired effect of helping you to unburden yourselves, even if only of your defenses. Or ignorance. For we are simply come among you in the humblest of capacities. Strictly here to call forth The Magic.

That being The Magic Of Love, the last pure thing left unsullied by the vulgarities of this world. Though often now cloaked in one or more of its many mysterious disguises, or defenses if you like that term better.

To you good people gathered around, where-and-whenever this time and place is, as we were most surely drawn up into The Ether by some thing or some one or another. And no longer seem at all able to recall the particulars of our said hastily made departures.

(sotto voice) Other than that lately I've been running

on faith. For what else can a poor boy do, to purloin a phrase.

TRANSIT:
He moves yet further right toward Eli, glancing timidly and furtively in that direction as if trying to telegraph his dire distress. Eli stands realizing Michael is either totally lost or has gotten entirely overwhelmed. As if sensing the same problem, Zackery stands and hurriedly crosses down to stop on Michael's left side.

MICHAEL:
(sotto voice) So all of you may gain Knowledge I was saying, by seeing face to face or eye to eye.

ZACKERY:
Anywho. Since we've never claimed to have divined the final answers, you sitting out there will not tonight be subjected to a ritualized working over by the 'we know it all so let us tell you how to live your lives' cudgel.

Oh no most dear new friends. Nor would we be first to cast stones among you, less some come back this direction. For we do so love our addled heads intact.

Not to mention excusing our occasional indulgences into the lesser carnal pleasures, such as wines and foods and cigars and the arts. As all including each of you must sometimes do, if for no reason other than to temporarily quiet those whispered cravings.

TRANSIT:
Eli sits again relieved, as Zackery shifts Michael a bit toward the left. Who attempts moving behind as if to hide. Putting a reassuring hand on Michael's arm Zackery pulls him forward, preparing to hand the proceedings back to his management again as soon as possible.

ZACKERY:
But know you that what we will do is converse a little. Speaking the words as penned, ever-so trippingly off the tongue. To try if we might, to open the locked shutters of your minds somewhat wider so to say.

In order to let stream in a bit more necessary sight. Thereby somewhat relieving your inner-most fears. And perhaps even banishing the monsters under your beds in favor of angels' hands on your heads.

But we best get down to it now. Because from the looks of you it's sooner started soonest done. While we still have you somewhat bedazzled, and before what passes for your natural wisdom begins to settle back in again.

For you see dears, we would not like the tar and feathers. Oh no. Not to mention our greater joy at not having to slink out of such a place as this, until the time we may decide to up and make said lingering departure.

TRANSIT:
Eli stands and crosses behind them to lean against the wall on the left. After gesturing a 'you got this' sort of flourish to Michael, Zackery turns and moves up to again sit in the row of chairs.

MICHAEL:
Ahem. As I suppose you have every right to expect how I should actually begin, I will with - verily it is said unto thee:

Hindsight. Blindsight. Think thou see-est? Mayhap yay or nay, but through a glass darkly. Foresight, poor sight. Blind in the light with malice toward none and all.

Same is always same, to wit to see any sight. Giving over to knowing The Magic thou might-st say? But ah, therein lies the rub. Better plucking out the eye than give offense, yet somehow me-thinks not. Far better to re-train this vision.

Doth protest too much silly foolish mortals. For import is crystal clear if thou would-st but try. Eye of raptor sees, mayhap directly into thine very soul. Could-st thou only focus one could see as well.

The stick out of thine eye and there sharpest vision. Light and Dark thus balance. By ducking between shadows, now thou might-st see.

TRANSIT:
He turns to pointedly look at Eli, who nods

approvingly and feigning casualness sits at the front left. Michael seems to sense his sweet spot is arriving and perhaps hits full stride, moving somewhat more to the right.

MICHAEL:
Enough already. For in The High Speech we have now proven some degree of ability. And aside from the simple fact that it's nowadays pretty much incomprehensible, in trying to keep that up we could hurt our speaking parts.

So now. Above the ground is how you learned to perceive everything must be. But that all is simply ungrounded would surely be much more apt. As the former implies something grand or noble in scope, while the latter shows the real face of it very much more clearly.

For there's nothing worthy of praise in most beginnings. And on the converse some endings are mean, bitter and even loathsome. So that first five minutes you've seen is only a fleeting glimpse, which doesn't even faintly reflect the true nature of the beast.

Oh, that five are wonderful while they light up The Universe. But they burn out much too quickly for the effort required to reproduce them. Still though your bad times even at their worst can be better than some will ever get to have.

And isn't that a strange concept in itself, that we

have to do such a qualifying thing? Even so it stands to reason that most bad days you'll ever have could still be above average. Though that isn't at all what you had in mind back when you started out on your journeys.

In truth of fact I'd have to say you didn't really have any clues upon which to begin your search. But just looked around as you went, at what things might be made to do.

Then desperately held onto whatever fitted while throwing out other bits when they didn't work. And ended up where you are Here and Now, mostly by not remembering how you got from There.

TRANSIT:
Eli stands and crosses to sit in an empty one of the row of chairs as Michael sits at the front right. But he stands and moves behind this chair almost immediately, so in concern Eli stands and moves to stand behind him. Michael pauses until Eli gives him a 'go on' motion.

MICHAEL:
So it wasn't as much by sweat of the brow as it was simple compromises to situations. Merely combining various bits and pieces to create something that never was before, and never will then be exactly so again.

But that wouldn't be for lack of The Knowledge on how to do whatever. Let's say it's a desire to let a thing stand and be celebrated for its oneness. Or maybe from not wishing to clone the real article. As if it never could be improved upon, something like would only call for comparison.

But it's interesting how distance tempers views. As one could almost convince one's self that anything is better than it actually is, when seen from a long way away. So what for the rest of today and the long string of years out there? Well, answers don't always come so cleanly when the questions are so nasty.

And nobody ever gets to just skate by without having to hold the dirty end of the stick. But what is there to do except go on taking steps along The Path? As there is only one direction in which you're enabled to go.

There's no turning back to choose again, and no re-doing of the missed or messed-up stuff. For you should by now be using all you have in building new upon those old foundations. And at that point there's also not being sure any of it should or could be sifted out in another fashion.

TRANSIT:
Zackery and Sienna stand almost in unison and cross to join Michael one on each side as he moves to the front center of the stage. Eli stands and moves behind them to lean against the wall on the left.

MICHAEL:
Because if that last five minutes was a bit beyond

just good compared to many or most, then maybe the next five will also be pretty much okay too.

SIENNA:
And anyway what choice is there? For it's not like you'll ever get even a fleeting ghost of a chance to change The Grand Plan's rules as you go on your way.

ZACKERY:
And a good thing that is too. For how else would you then ever decide exactly where the out of bounds line is?

TRANSIT:
Michael takes one each of their hands and joins them. Then turns, crossing to sit in the row of chairs. Eli moves to stand behind them as they face each other, seems to think better of it and slowly goes to sit in the chair at the right front of the stage.

ZACKERY:
It was The Love.

SIENNA:
Which became our Love once we gave over to being tangled in the wire.

ZACKERY:
This one with emerald eyes took my life by entering it. For then I was helplessly falling relentlessly ever upward through the sky-rift's first split, to peer into that new dawn. Past stars lighted by your passing

while hurtling to lovingly embrace that which was secretly entreated.

When just to know you'd whispered. At that final witness line if you will, on which I ran dry of places to hide. Unarmed and without will to resist, defenses being no longer valid. For everything seemed ordained.

And you simply drew deepest breath, intending yet another scream into the face of yonder beast. But it was again too soon. So you patiently waited instead for the do all, save all, end all you wished us to discover.

SIENNA:
This one with emerald eyes believed it was always possible. So I revised the criteria down to perhaps a thousand centuries, then to a thousand selected decades. But settled on the final thousand years which would mean most to us in retrospect.

For the heart once set beating its time must be turned free. Taking flight to stick exactly where it may or must, after rebounding from the myriad impostures. I'd set mine to strike full-force the intended target of you.

Ripping deeply to release the vital essences to splatter on the floor in red rain of liberation. Until we must lift our robes a bit higher, temporarily avoiding the crimson. Into which I wantonly stepped.

Allowing myself better sight of the roots feasting therein, as they consumed their fair share of the planned-to-diminish flow trickling down from our voluntarily incurred wounds. Accepted in best defense of this perceived last romantic realm.

ZACKERY:
That one with emerald eyes is the true mask of reason I chose to wear daily. But I asked pardon then if you could or would. For Madame had taken me wrongly even as I heard those first tentative words tumble out.

Was never my intent to inflict offense, and certainly not to provoke. As why would any practicing poet risk the peril of offending his muse? Far better to rather curry your favor than to be kicked to the curb, wordless.

So I timidly asked, dearest lady for what are you here requiring I share now? Last life-blood or simply verbal expressions? Well to either or both as is your right, for I only await to make humblest offerings to you.

SIENNA:
I with emerald eyes am forever leaping into the vastness as guardian against the deadly Darkness along with him. But then a new world for us both was imagined within our fair sight. Into which we only fleetingly glimpsed from our temporal but necessary perches high on the buttes overlooking the desert's vastness.

Then after the walls fell but before the reentry burn began, came an emotional storm. Even a hurricane of physicality for us all. In whose eye we took residence on Someday. Bereft upon the coldest slate floor, conjured as a willing prison.

Never daring raise sight toward the coffered mirror, fearful of our selves staring back. Disdainfully accusing of not enough sincere worth to earn the raw salt required for self-preservation, let alone sufficient amounts to offer spice to others.

ZACKERY:
Then life itself was loosed from inside you, as living it was released from me. So we came down from There to Here. The drawing of those needed by the twins was completed and Wulfsgate made real and solid.

Now even after all was thought heard by mankind, there is yet promise of the delicate sound of distant thunder in our velvet Love, for those willing to seek its source.

Upon this recovery I now plaintively plead: Oh once after some far distant gale yet to come, might I be so profoundly privileged as to still be eternally lost in your Love. By what grace The Keepers might dain see fit.

Until on the final Someday morning when every change has happened and we prepare to depart one last time, joyously dying in each others arms. May there still be only the whispered whispers of you, with emerald eyes.

TRANSIT:
They embrace warmly and hold each other until Michael stands and crosses to the center between them as they split. Eli stands and moves behind them to lean against the wall on the left.

MICHAEL:
So why would these two have drawn focus to that Here?

SIENNA:
This was The Love.

ZACKERY:
This is our Love.

ZACKERY & SIENNA:
Make this your Love.

TRANSIT:
They turn and cross to sit in the row of chairs. Michael begins moving right, glancing at Eli who sits on the left. But he suddenly moves back toward the center. So Eli stands and crosses behind him, pausing to throw an untrustworthy look at his back. He then continues right to lean against the wall.

MICHAEL:
And for that matter exactly how could and should anyone? Well clearly not by ones self alone. But with

each bound to the other by the choicest of ties, perhaps not even necessarily of conscious processes.

And most certainly not resultant from as has been said, sinning in haste to repent at leisure. For notice that the barbed wires within which they have tangled themselves appear very well embedded.

Then marvel how the new creature grew that well while so leashed. So let's propose that other than mankind in general being chastened, none specifically protested or even noticed The Dark's impact but the ones left behind wondering about the sun.

For it wasn't likely the one staggered into the others blindly in the thousand years of lingering dimness. Not forgetting to take account of where we had begun, for you must see there's always a definitive jump-off point.

As witness that even the world's finest root-stock thrives most or best just after when a required pruning to allow for an intended graft occurs.

But what if some choices made during that murkiness weren't the best of which you were capable, even granted unforeseen options or not-known-to-be available resources? If so, an awful lot of wasted water flowed over that particular dam without notable benefit.

Surely how one's synapses were encoded in

childhood comes into play, plus or minus in-grown value systems and sound judgment. As those depend upon learning lessons best illustrated by prime exhibits and examples of excellent familiar behavior.

Allowing for using one's mind to the fullest extent possible. Freely roaming depths, breadths or heights previously unknown. But all the while not shirking the responsibilities tied to those aforementioned concepts. Far better to be measured through trial and tribulation than settle complacently inside another's box.

For to have so done, would be to never know your truth. And that brand of truth Is what defines the possible well as the "im" equally.

Even if discovered light-weight or wanting, no doubt could or would be left as to projected functionability. As after all it's only the sincere-est fools who can truly fly before actually falling. So dare to be fully grown beyond any and all traditional bounds, becoming better whoever whatever however.

As there's no intrinsic value in not re-inventing the wheel every day. For after done is done, nothing cleaves so cleanly as a virgin, though also un-tried but therefore un-sullied blade. And life-lessons launched off such a bloody tip cannot be discounted.

TRANSIT:
Sophia stands and crosses to join Michael on his left as Eli sits at the right front. She hugs him who reacts

shocked, turning to look at Eli while crossing up to the row of chairs. She moves to sit at the left front as Eli stands and crosses to stand behind her. Michael turns to stare at their backs just before sitting.

MICHAEL:
But perhaps it bodes better to become remolded at key contact points. To enable better sight of exactly what works and of what just doesn't do squat.

SOPHIA:
The view through differing eyes offers true omniscient vision. Whether the old ones be blinded by masking or else denial, a bit of blood or even spit in -might serve as clarification.

So let us and you make a pact together, right Here and right Now. To leave those horrible things over which we have little or no actual control anyway, alone to take care of themselves. However that may happen.

Though I know first-hand that relinquishing eons-long control isn't easy, as it goes against the grain. Giving us however, much more free time to go out or stay in. To play at painting and words and sculpture and music or other fanciful arts.

Without making those terrifically mournful cares of the world so much our own. Should not be that terribly difficult a thing for us to do you know? As this careful letting go of our possibly mis-begotten responsibilities is what allows Magic to begin.

Well as, this far removed we were never that sure why we became so concerned with those people and their places and these things — that were probably not our problems after all. So perhaps Love really is all with which we've ever needed to learn to deal.

TRANSIT:
She stands and moves to the front center of the stage as Eli follows. Elise stands and crosses down to the left front watching Sophia with apparent great respect.

SOPHIA:
And probably if they knew our deepest worries or the cares we'd developed on their behalf, their laughter would surely drown out our wailing at their injustice to us away.

All said and done, perhaps we each would have been better off not trying to become self-appointed saviors of a world that didn't need or want saving. And some knew their business anyway, as shouldn't we all?

If only in order to say truth when professing that we know Love. For we certainly wouldn't want the pressure a comparison to what life was like before our current Someday occurred would heap upon us.

ELISE:
Besides, if we look back to what some supposed

future histories will say purportedly happened to Them, not a single one of us could handle the responsibility for making those decisions regarding mankind.

TRANSIT:
Sophia crosses to the left to take both of Elise's hands, then kisses her cheek. Eli moves to sit in the chair at front right while Sophia crosses to the row of chairs and sits as Elise pauses, a bit flustered.

ELISE:
Love is not, cannot be the end all save all do all, for which you might wish it to be. For in spite of, or in addition to your cover story, there really is a reality out There. Lives change, dreams fail, and some things just don't or won't work as planned.

So one may not ever get all the way to where it's intended to finish. But that's not really that big a deal when The Path is finally at ends. The act of having genuinely tried to apply The Magic Of Love is what matters most at the last.

Along the way you will have touched many and been touched by them, as all contact begins and ends with a reaction. Which in turn causes others.

TRANSIT:
Michael stands, crosses down to the right front of the stage and pauses watching Elise, as Eli stands to move and stop behind him.

ELISE:
This Love you must share cannot vanish long as at least one star which was passed remembers. This swing through The Universe brushes by many, so you're safe there.

That which you'll do and say and be is all one could ever dare ask for anyway. It's what spreads like dust in the wind and ends up in everybody's eye. So they all have the opportunity to really and finally see.

TRANSIT:
As if without thinking about it she turns and blows Michael a flirty little kiss across the stage. He moves to the center while making a 'caught it' gesture as Elise turns and almost struts up to sit in an empty chair of the row. Eli leans against the wall on the right.

MICHAEL:
This thing. This demon in velvet, loves to be held against a heaving chest. Certain it controls what? Some thing, some one, some Other, some object of affection? Little does it know a reality like having energy sapped or cares of such things, until it is much too late.

But by then we'll have been everywhere in its dozing head, having cooked dozens of its own murder of crows in butter pies sans its Knowledge.

But those bodies such as you have Here are for doing that dance which celebrates swimming against tides. And learning to etch stone produces smoother surfaces upon which to reflect and concentrate The Magic Of Love.

Until ungrounded yet still firmly planted, you writhe as lovers beneath the cloud sheets. Which scorches Terra itself. Thereby coming around at long last to understand the naked truth of this and other matters. Perchance to use these new skills in mythical proportions.

TRANSIT:
He moves toward the right and turns to give Eli a rather strange sharp look. Who sits in the front right chair dismissively, as Sienna stands and crosses down to the front center watching Michael a bit uneasily.

MICHAEL:
And what then of those whom you've lost? How to move into a mode other than pause, or then again maybe to just not. But history says you must so it can be guessed that you will. As take my word, Never is not really very long.

What of those whom you've lost? Moving on pretends to be normal, that pretense being what is required. As others' worry is lessened by presenting the brave but fake face.

For the best defense is done by the world's great mimes. With how greasepaint looks and not how true words sound apparently being what living is thought to be about. By them or they.

Those whom you've lost? Oh they're on display almost every day, as mannequins hold up well in The Light. Though the non-blinking thing gives them away if one stares hard enough. Surprising how many are encountered on a slow walk across the showroom floor.

SIENNA:
Whom you've lost? Not lost so much as just deactivated. Hurts a lot less when the numbness grows doesn't it? But even if you dim the lights all the way down to only a glow, there's still more than enough sight to understand how it must go, according to The Tangle.

TRANSIT:
Michael turns and goes to sit in an empty chair of the row. Zackery stands and quickly crosses to join Sienna on her left, as Eli stands and moves up to sit in another empty chair of the row near Michael.

SIENNA:
You have been warned that there are writers, shine down a lighters, to enable some sighters. You have been warned that there are speakers, real truth seekers, better take a peekers.

ZACKERY:
You have been warned that there are singers, something for you bringers, draw attention by

stingers. You have been warned that there are players, settle in and stayers, show you another wayers.

SIENNA:
You have been warned that there are dancers, make a little romancers, and why not take a stancers. You have been warned that there are performers, cannot be conformers, another way reformers.

ZACKERY:
You have been warned that there are coulders, anyone who thinks woulders, know that you really shoulders. But you were never told or taught that these are the true artists. And that it is them and their works which make your lives worth the living.

TRANSIT:
Sophia stands and crosses down to the stage's front center to stop between them. Sienna and Zackery hug her and cross to the row of chairs to sit, just as Eli stands and moves to stand behind her.

SOPHIA:
As that for some inexplicably sad reason, has been rather sorely left for you each to figure out - alone where and when you sat There in The Dark.

TRANSIT:
All freeze for a slow fade to black and Intermission.

AGAINST THE BLACK-CHROME SUN: ACT TWO

TRANSIT:
A slow fade up from black to exactly the same setting and actor placement as was shown before the intermission.

SOPHIA:
And so what dear darling people, what is there left that can be said for embracing The Magic Of Love? As choosing to believe it not leaves one uselessly stranded in the shadowed Wasteland.

While giving over to the tangled wire of its belief bathes you in the purest Light. Options on that huh? No, for us. As love I and still love they, that glow of it so much.

Now listen sharply. You'll have to agree that by involving you as our witnesses we've become increasingly more intimate during this evening. Until we've now reached the time for last confession, and perhaps even of final absolution.

Oh no. No no no. Only Michael's, for we could never dare require such a delicate thing of you. Any of your buried secrets are strictly matters best kept between you and your hearts far as we're concerned.

TRANSIT:
In thought, she slowly moves to sit at the right front of the stage. Eli comes to hover behind her chair as

Michael stands and crosses down front to the center. Eli turns to stare hard at him, which is ignored.

SOPHIA:
But in the interest of truth his remaining veil must be parted, exposing the last core of himself. For you to see plainly from where he has come and of what he speaks. That you may know the true depth of feelings surrounding the import of what we're sharing with you here tonight.

Also of our sincere care and concern for every one of you seekers who have gathered here expecting to receive a little something more, as you shall. And after all, everyone's history is actually their current Now when done will be done in the future.

TRANSIT:
She stands and crosses to the center to put one hand on Michael's cheek and kiss his other. He turns in amazement to watch her glide toward the row of chairs to sit, as Eli sits at the right front. Michael moves across the stage to sit at the left front and pauses in reflection.

MICHAEL:
Sitting alone by choice on a beach in a summer sunset. Now There only in tow while they've come to clear my father's stuff and such. Who'd lied. Saying he'd see me again soon, just a couple of months before he chose The Clearing at the end of The Path instead.

Wish I'd known he'd already made such decision not to linger Here in life longer. Doubt that at such tender age I'd have imagined good enough ways to mend his broken heart and head, but perhaps I would've paid better attention to the real and neat things he often had to say.

TRANSIT:
Eli stands and very slowly moves to the front center. He carefully sits on the floor so as not to interrupt Michael, all the while watching him intently.

MICHAEL:
Now I've got to move upbeach a bit, saving my little pile of papers from another tide. Which I hadn't noticed until today that life within Love's Magic is exactly like that cycle. Coming and going seemingly at will, to bring in or take out whatsoever it may.

But don't pity when I pout that it's perhaps taken out more than it's brought in so far. As I'll get by and be better off too, soon as I can begin to start to be able to understand anything more clearly that is.

TRANSIT:
Eli almost reverently slides a bit more left as if needing to be even closer to Michael. Who turns right to stare at him, as if having just noticed Eli sitting nearby and speaks directly only to him.

MICHAEL:
The nightmare of that Wolf I can't seem to let go of

now. He's come each night the last few months, yet still hasn't actually gotten me. But he's always out there, stalking the same fields time after time. Nipping my heels to let me know he could take me whenever but hasn't bothered.

Just sort of trotting along and play-growling to gain my attention by shaking aware grief-deadened wit and nerve, and probably when I came full-blown to life-long codependence with what's now termed post traumatic stress disease.

Fast-forward a way down or up The Path to another time very distant. On very different sand and a very different beach, but against the very same sunset again. This time sorting out the leftovers of yet another life lost too soon. Wallowing in the wake of departure generated by That Time's dear mate.

TRANSIT:
Eli suddenly grimaces and turns himself away to the right as if not wanting to have to see whatever pain Michael is remembering. Michael turns back to face the house and pauses to re-gather himself.

MICHAEL:
And I couldn't even blame her for not knowing this was a battle she wouldn't win. That other powers had already made that decision in her stead. As if They ran out of enough good reasons for her to stay, rather than go on to a new whatever wherever.

More and different papers to shift upbeach to save from the incoming of that same ocean. And The Magic Of Love has grown within me during many quick years of ebbing and flowing tides. Much time spent giving, getting and sharing it all, still mostly without satisfactory explanations though.

But there's no longer any pouting now about the losses, even though that still works just like it always has. Learning to grow and change and adapt finally allows me to stare boldly straight Ahead, almost unflinchingly.

TRANSIT:
Michael stands and crosses toward the center to pause and turn toward Eli as if intending to speak directly to him again. But he continues to the right to sit instead. Eli stands and turns to watch him rather helplessly.

MICHAEL:
As to The Wolf? Still here. Not starring in dark nightmares anymore, but in lovely Technicolor dreams. Seems he'd come to protect and teach rather than harass. Least since the time I lost it and screamed at him to just take me or else cut it the freak out, once I finally got lost courage remembered.

And in these later adventures he even runs into Sandburg's old front parlor right along with me when I come in from an evening playing at poetry and/or capturing fireflies. So he's become my most boon companion both day and night.

Though on the odd rare occasions he does go his own way, probably designed to periodically leave me on my own. So he can see how I'll do when he has to be away, in attendance Elsewhere or Elsetime for The Keepers.

TRANSIT:
Eli moves right across the stage to stand behind Michael's chair, who stands wearily and moves center as Eli sits in that now vacant place. Michael pauses staring hard over his shoulder off to the right side of the stage before turning back to face the house.

MICHAEL:
One more blink ahead or behind in the journey leads to a much more realistically current version of my self. And still again it's the same sunset, but now over the myriad sands from all the innumerable beaches on which I've been privileged to sit and ponder. And even to perhaps write my wrongs.

Beginning yet another chapter of living exactly how a life should flow in toto. This time setting every detail down in ink by my own hand into a single volume rather than on random loose paper scraps. So those still coming along The Path behind me may have something interesting to follow via my ramblings and meanderings.

Then quite unexpectedly a bagpiper and fireworks on the shoreline heralded The True Queen's return to rule over The Universe again. She and I have decided by mutual blood-agreement that none has option to check out early during this particular version of our romp through the stars.

One time more, a probable close to last saving of my now tome upbeach from the restlessly timeless tide. This part of the journey toward Love's Magic having clearly shown me once and for all in exquisite minutia exactly what the feast of life is really supposed to be about.

Seems it evens out and works exactly as should, If I can simply somehow manage to leave it the hell alone until The Tapestry finishes weaving its self tight. With meaning to be at the very crux of what makes all the difference in what I encounter while stumbling through the experiences of Here.

For surely it's far better to see and experience a bit of it all and then exercise at least some of the many options, than to have simply only sat contentedly but stupidly in the rancid mud of what might have otherwise been.

TRANSIT:
Eli stands and crosses to the front center as Michael turns to speak to only him again. He then turns back to face the house as Eli steps slightly behind him, now intently looking off to the right side of the stage.

MICHAEL:

Oh Monsieur Wolf? He literally marked me with his brand here, more than a few years back. Said it was to help me remember that he's grown into an astounding maturity, as well as have I. Both now disconnectedly far from the Wile E. Coyote cartoon model with which we'd began.

And recently we came damned-close to entering The Clearing at the end of The Path when They bet our heart on showing that there's deadly seriousness in the lessons we've shared on life and applying The Magic. And even on the fine art of losing well.

Guess we passed those tests, since we get to continue Here. Though remembering how to be completely still head-wise, is now as always the hardest thing to do as I strive to achieve what he expects of me each new day.

But his promise of The Wulfyre to always light and lengthen my way along any storm-darkened pathway, gives me pause.

TRANSIT:

Eli abruptly turns back to look at him as Michael makes a paw-like fist with his uplifted left hand, holding it overhead and staring up at it. As if without thought Eli does the very same gesture at almost the very same time.

MICHAEL:

Gives me paws.

TRANSIT:
Eli moves to and puts his arm around Michael's waist as they turn to cross to the chairs at centerstage. Michael stops in front of them staring very hard right and then clumsily sits. Eli looks to the right himself and pauses as if concerned, then moves left to stand behind the chairs while turning to stare at Michael.

ELI:
(sotto voice) Michael, you see what's yonder don't you?

MICHAEL:
Oh my darling dears. We are uhm, I am most surely ah, momentarily flailing. Apparently unexpectedly almost done-in by laboring under the uhm, unrelenting emotional burden of expressing what you were warranted to hear and learn Here tonight. Yes, that's all, sure.

It would apparently seem that in our ah, my zeal to start this evening I have inadvertently neglected to secure upon my immediate personage the properly required libation. Or drink in the local vernacular, to provide for adequate lubrication of the speaking parts thereof.

In yet another phraseology my throat is dry as dust, and I more than require some wine or ale. Even as last resort though forbid, water. But in lieu of any of that out here I am of necessity relenting to the tiniest break from the stage, to quench.

(sotto voice) As well as to peer a bit further into ... that.

TRANSIT:
Eli moves to stand behind Michael's chair, concerned. Who turns to look off right yet again as The Company turn as one to follow his stare. Michael suddenly stands and reaches to take Elise's hand, who complacently stands in confusion at what is suddenly taking place.

He crosses to the center front of the stage with Elise in tow. Eli moves behind them, hovering anxiously. Then Michael seems to somewhat recover and momentarily once again becomes the stagemaster in charge. He bows to Elise and turns to address the house.

MICHAEL:
So now without any further dilly-dallying or lollygagging on my part. Here for your consideration, contemplation and hopefully also your consternation - once again, this incomparable one. To head our performance expediently on toward its barn of completion.

My darling the stage is all. All yours that is. And there, your most willing and yet unwitted witnesses. Have at it.

TRANSIT:
Elise withdraws her hand and takes a step left, as he pivots to look and point at her dramatically. Eli

crosses to and sits at the front left to watch this unfold. Michael moves toward the chairs looking right again, to stop in front of the row.

He staggers as Sophia and Sienna stand in alarm. He waves them away and they sit as he unsteadily exits at the center back of the stage, while Eli watches after him.

Elise distractedly crosses more left clearly disturbed, and pauses to compose herself. Eli stands and moves to stand just behind her shoulder. She turns to look as if somehow sensing him there, then turns back forward.

ELISE:
(sotto voice) It was long-ago written that when The Dark and The Light merged into a single new beast on Someday, the resultant gray showed only as if shadows. So release was granted, allowing for Sienna's colors to thrive.

Therefore happily everafter exists though only hindsight might prove it so. But out this far from your starting points and with tomorrow still yet a distance, your final and forever coupling fits almost perfectly.

So perch fearlessly here on the precipice, wishing either to fall or fly. For any choices my darlings are after all only choices, though often of greatest import. Or else there's simply no reason and therefore nothing at all.

Such rightness must make the stand in plain sight as you ramble and meander on side by side. For as one may somewhere go so then must the other also, with none untangling to leave The Path early. Unless some grand unseen Other wills it thusly.

TRANSIT:
She slowly moves back to the front center of the stage, speaking even more confidently - as if knowing this is finally her prime time. Eli crosses to and sits on the left, seemingly content to simply watch and admire her work.

ELISE:
But our best survival even while tangled in this wire requires some detachment, or at least the banishment of heedless over-reacting. While yet grounded in the firmament of being grown deeply unrepeatable. And so onward together past time's end. In witness of that blood slicks the floor, with your footprints marking the procession.

For as all was, all is and must be indefinitely. Defending past last breath this truth. By deciding to decide or else deciding to not, with that decision then defining all else. As either living or existing, while both belong to the larger Etre' by having similar motions involved, still illustrate their selves in vast differences.

So go on lighting stars as you pass to flash-fill the blank black spaces. First creating no new harm, though your creating in and of itself is a prime. Oh.

But even star shine may be too harsh upon your gentle faces, much less fair sunlight in those newly un-blinded eyes.

Then once more with reckless abandon into that yawning breach you'll run with us to lunge heart-first, as of course must be done. Only needing barely enough sight to stumble the way forward.

TRANSIT:
She moves slightly left as Eli stares off right past her. She reverses herself and glides back to the center smoothly to pause. Eli abruptly changes his focus to watch her even more intently.

ELISE:
But certain sacrifices do as they simply must, come into play. And one must be dedicatedly willing to give all one has when that is the requirement to make most clear one's point.

In this case being: A life without Love, is worth even less than no life at all.

And this is what you begged for, as if this is what you needed. So here is what you wanted, loving and loathing. Dreams lie scattered. The smoke is dispersed.

But with a mirror now held in front, allowing you to see clearly what lies behind. So take in all that's been done, to know what yet needs doing.

And this is what you begged for, as if this is what you needed. So here is what you wanted, loving and loathing. Heed that dark reflection. The real thing in gory detail.

But not yet etched into history, as change is still a possibility. Evolving or else devolving to become the more enlightened ones.

(sotto voice) Steeling myself for this end-act. Always an awful shock even when expecting it. Detesting the absolute necessity of how this example must go.

TRANSIT:
She creeps forward toward the stage's leading edge, locking eyes with each member of the house as Eli gets caught up, standing and staring enthralled.

ELISE:
And this is what gets paid, as this is what's been earned. Witness the reward of not truly learning, but only loathing not loving.

So Here, you shall one way or the other have what you're bloody-well seeking. Then be gone, as I'll be so done with you. Having offered you teat to suckle far better than that for which you came, or perhaps deserve.

And there is no more cold comfort to be had here in my utter and abject failure, I croak between drawn lips. For then must I die by hanging from the cruel rope. Having been uncontestedly convicted guilty of being, of being Loveless.

TRANSIT:
As if on cue Eli suddenly slams his foot on the floor mimicking the sound of a trapdoor, as Elise falls limply to the stage. She pauses before slowly raising her head and propping her chin on her hands to stare openly at the house.

ELISE:
Drawing eyelids down hatch-tight I cloak myself in imagined invisibility in vain attempt to hide my well-earned shame and dishonor.

But for those still uncertain few in the dispersing throng among you, who will dare glance over hunched shoulders, fearing yet yearning to know if there is one final retort?

My abandoned corpse only swings oh-so slowly to and fro in silhouette, against the black-chrome sun. Beneath the canted and creaking gallows poles upon which I've been hoisted to hang countless times before.

As ravens feast among scattered bread crusts cast beneath my boots to lure them in. A more perverse part of your crowd hoping they'd finish me in their feeding-frenzy. Though thus-far each has disdained to partake, as has not so my sacrificial side.

Those clever clever birds perhaps sensing such

tainted meat as I could well be their last supper,
and not willing to give all for maybe naught as have
I.

TRANSIT:
Eli spontaneously steps to the stage's center offering
a helping hand to her. Who takes it without thought
and stands unsteadily. She then realizes what has
just happened and pauses, openly gawking joyously
at him.

ELISE:
(sotto voice) Eli?

TRANSIT:
He nods, does a minor flourish and almost shows a
grin while moving to lean right against the wall as if
satisfied. It dawns on The Company that for the first
time they too actually see Eli, and all but Zackery
react almost as one in gasping, pointing and staring
at him.

SOPHIA:
(sotto voice) He is real, which must mean that The
Magic Of Love is real too. Oh this proves everything.

TRANSIT:
Elise smiles dazzlingly in his direction before turning
back to once more face forward.

ELISE:
Then shaking off the stiffness within my not weak,
but only weary flesh, I again slip the well-worn, well-

trusted noose from around my oh-so very practiced throat. And take momentary pause, floating high above the lynching-place stage. Then softly settle back to the word-crusted killing field.

TRANSIT:
Michael enters from the center of the back of the stage and moves to pause behind the chairs while always looking right. But he turns back acknowledging the reactions to Eli's reveal, and slowly crosses to stop and hover behind Elise. Eli tries to wave him away, but is ignored.

ELISE:
Well-contented with the overly-graphic lesson I've provided you, I who knows my self in this moment only as 'that wretched woman' - cackle a well-earned absolution, before my next performance in this little freak show laughingly called Love.

Turning then, I

MICHAEL:
(steps on line) Hold. Oh hold here. For the Love of all that's Lovely, hold most dear Elise.

TRANSIT:
She is thrown off and misses a beat while stumbling a step left, shocked and staring at him in disbelief. Eli crosses behind them to the left of the stage and stops. The Company stands almost in unison and crosses down to gather around Michael, Elise and Eli.

ZACKERY:
Michael? Eli? What the Dickens, she's not done

ELI:
(steps on line) Yes, she is Zackery.

SOPHIA:
Oh come on Michael. Eli, he's gone off-script

ELI:
(steps on line) No, he hasn't Sophia.

SIENNA:
But Michael. Eli, surely

ELI:
(steps on line) Hold Sienna.

MICHAEL:
Oh, begging forgiveness am I darling Elise. And from you all dear Company, but it's warranted.

TRANSIT:
Elise forcefully pushes Michael away to the right and moves angrily left. Eli suddenly firmly in control of the events moves center and raises his hands for everyone to hold. They freeze. Michael crosses to Elise and speaks to her with his back to all else, as she tries to ignore him.

MICHAEL:
(sotto voice) Don't be cross with me sweetheart, as that I could not bear. It breaks my heart to interrupt

you dear. But I'll sincerely supplicate later, if need be.

TRANSIT:
Michael pauses and snaps back to face front when Eli taps his shoulder and points right. He and The Company turn to look. Michael and Eli move to the front center as the rest of The Company turn as one and cross to sit in the row of chairs. Eli nods pointedly at Michael and moves left to lean uneasily against the wall.

ELI:
Hear him now most loved friends. Gather in quick and listen close, or whatever.

MICHAEL:
While I was offstage, I heard Elise build toward her close and steeled myself for the end-act though expecting it. Loathing the necessity. During which I chanced to again glance sky-ward reflectingly into or at least toward those grandly re-colored heavens.

Dumbstruck, I was none-the-less uh, convicted to return here and redirect you away from the dramatic example and astounding lesson she was leading you toward. But trust your good cousin hard on this one.

That what I have glimpsed there clearly indemnifies this unfortunate disruption of our oh-so carefully planned proceedings. And gives us every reason to take redirective pause, as you will come to understand.

For my dears I have seen the next great cosmic gale, which is taking aim to come down full-force on us. Meaning that yet another Someday is not far off. And while it is yet still out there a way, you must none the less rest assured that it is coming most soon.

Now, we all love the good storms, do we not? As they serve to stir and clear the air, both literally and figuratively. But this darlings, is a very very bad one. As it need be in order to serve both Time and Function of The Keepers Grand Plan.

And this one will most probably also bring back the full yellow Light, as was foretold before the old walls ever fell. So it's come nye unto time to scatter. Time to duck and cover your heads. Time to draw loved ones close. Time to implement, survival. Even as our scant time among you draws short.

For yet again have we been humbled. Foiled in getting to decide when to take our casual leave from some loving place, though The Continuum knows we do so abhor keeping to a schedule. Perhaps that's our personal take-away point from Here.

TRANSIT:
He notices Eli waving and pointing right once again for him to move things along, nods at him, looks right himself and turns back front. Eli crosses to join him at the front and center of the stage. They turn together to address remarks to only The Company.

ELI:
And most apologetically we say to you dears, start to commence to begin to unfurl the tarps. And cinch them down tightly over our stage, our hearth and our heart Here. Where the roads have marked with their crossing our little ripple of enlightenment.

Where it's doggedly hoped that somewhere in between the myriad darks and dawns to which we've been privy, the true seekers out there will have seen or heard from the determination of our labors just how to embrace Love again. Or else we have had no reason.

TRANSIT:
Michael turns back to face the house as Eli moves slightly to stand just behind his left shoulder.

MICHAEL:
But now all of you there must go, and hurry yourselves along to do what you can or will or need to prepare for what is coming next. Secure in knowing that there are brighter, better days on the yonder side of that which is pending.

As we remain Here a bit longer, tarrying a scant moment to softly curse perceived reality. As of course is our collective birthright, bought and paid in blood upon the page. So come family, come Tribe.

TRANSIT:
The Company stands and once again almost moves

as one, splitting and flanking Michael and Eli on each side.

ELI:
(sotto voice) Yet again, really?

Only us this band of wussie poets, yet again expected to make a stand against this coming maelstrom and of Love's Magic once again be sole defenders.

We, who hold no weaponry devices or last defenses but an unsharpened pen and these remanufactured hearts. Yet ordained to step up and spit directly into the face of the looming beast.

ZACKERY:
Which generates such withering criticism, completely whisking away any shred of validation in its wake. Except for what small parcels we may savor unto ourselves.

SIENNA:
Apparently this is the necessary sacrament, in order to dominate still another of the continuous battles in which we have engaged The Darkness.

SOPHIA:
But Michael, Eli and we all are on board for that. As our only stated goal while any where any time remains as ever to offer up even the balance of our Eternity for the sake of protecting and promoting The Magic Of Love.

ELISE:
That indeed seems the lot drawn for us. So once more into the yawning breach in defense of this perhaps last romantic realm. As these things we do to keep the flame burning, with which to write The Wulfyre in the sky.

MICHAEL:
So. Though tomorrow may never show either case, are we simply left to seek forgiveness in advance of our probable shortcoming? Or can we somehow finally begin to hope of actually saving them, much less our selves?

Have we achieved the sincere worth to earn even the minimum measure of raw salt required for our self-preservation? Let alone sufficient amounts to offer the spice of life to those others?

ELI:
So what say you dears?

SOPHIA:
We are good enough.

COMPANY:
That is truth.

ZACKERY:
And we have paid sufficient dues.

COMPANY:
And that is truth.

SIENNA:
We have the right.

COMPANY:
That is truth.

ELISE:
And it is our time.

COMPANY:
And we are the truth.

MICHAEL:
You there please helplessly hope as do we Players that we are strong enough to draw you all through to the other side, back into The Light we knew.

ELI:
By hoisting high our meager battle shield, though only a paper banner filled with words, up and over your heads.

COMPANY:
So say we one, so say we all.

TRANSIT:
The six all link hands, pause while looking at each other and split. All but Sophia turn and cross up to the row of chairs to sit randomly. She turns to look at them, turns back and moves to the front left to face forward again.

SOPHIA:
Oh we're still drifting at sea in that same leaky lifeboat. But now much better off since the jacks like those walls, like my walls, have tumbled. And while the blues will always cry on the face of the wind, there's still plenty left for the lunatics yet to come by our same path.

Now another view is set to shine brightly after this black-chrome sun. Mirrors, smoke and dreams being what were thankfully left us. And the relentless pursuit of that useless perfection was indeed found while strolling through the noise, as was predicted.

TRANSIT:
She sits in the chair on the left as Michael stands, crosses to stand behind her chair and puts his hands on her shoulders. Eli stands and moves to the right front part of the wall to lean there.

SOPHIA:
Having gone upstream to our very cores found much more than idle time and hands. And while certain fires dying did indeed cool some things a bit as required, perfect ignorance ignored complete perception.

Now you each well as I, know more of our inside selves too. So Sophia no longer has the need to maintain absolute separation to control action or attract affection. Outrageous, as doing it right has once more clearly proved the power of The Magic Of Love.

In this time of surviving, entire oceans were indeed experienced and examined one drop at a time. And by the way, boats invariably leak most exactly when we need them as they always have and always will.

But so far just as was said would be the case, all our marbles do at least seem to still be contained in that one basket we call Love.

TRANSIT:
She stands and moves to the front center, turns right to lock eyes with Eli, turns and looks left at Michael before facing front again. Staring up toward the theatre's ceiling she pauses, perhaps as if either repentant, or momentarily still unsure of herself.

Michael crosses to Eli at the front right and both turn to watch Sophia slowly cross toward the row of chairs to sit. She stands back up, takes a step forward and turns to The Company to speak a line. She then sits again as Michael and Eli cross to the center facing the house.

SOPHIA:
(sotto voice) I Love you each so very, very much.

ELI:
So Now dears kneel upon a figurative knee with us as if in literal benediction, Here in this soon to be un-quiet place. Where perhaps some small but still valid, old-world, yellow-sun Knowledge has been reborn tonight.

As we voice fondest wishes that you depart from your time with we humble Players here at Wulfsgate with something real taken away, hidden and held deep within yourselves. Perhaps the rekindled right to Love its self.

MICHAEL:
Now we release and beseech you with only destiny being our deliverance, to hurriedly take your leave. And to flee from this sticking-spot quickly as you may be so able, as there is no longer anything here for you to be had of us. For we have by now wholly and utterly run the voodoo down, Eli.

TRANSIT:
He nods to Eli and moves a step left. They begin turning to cross to where The Company sits. But Michael snaps back to address the house yet again. Eli openly grimaces, throws his hands in the air and comes back center attempting to hush Michael by putting a restraining hand on his arm.

MICHAEL:
Oh wait. Lingering to offer an offering as you will, for ours is but a hungry coffer begging to be fed. But only as you are led of course, as we've never been known to co-erce.

ELI:
Now we're finished. Well, except. The Wulfsgate Players bequeath you long days with pleasant nights. In truth twice the number you might have otherwise

had. And trust you've been helped a trifle more than you've been hindered or held back.

The black-chrome sun is not fixed, nor we all beneath it. At least until everything changes at the next Someday. But now you know what is known. So with our empty hands in our pockets and the dust of ages upon our boots, we'll simply turn and walk. Having offered all the comfort spared to share Here.

MICHAEL:
So, how do you? How do you like us now? But perhaps that's of little matter, as we'll tip our virtual glasses to you all anyway. So to borrow a line: make it one for our friends and one more for the road. That long long road.

This torch we hold must be displayed somewhere, Elsewhere. Or it soon might implode. So until we may chance meet in The Clearing at the end of The Path a time long hence:

TRANSIT:
Michael moves a bit more left, giving Eli some working room and nods in his direction.

ELI:
Those who hear not the music within these words we pen and must speak might think we dancers mad. But it's just exactly those same marvelous sounds which drive us, whirling upon this earth.

And long as we are spinning, none dare interrupt these steps. So hold tight that embrace as we go, whether vertical or lying down. As all isn't too much to ask for while right Here right Now.

Oh they? Well they won't understand these patterns until we show them what's inside us. So for today it's just we chosen few who are dancing as hard as we can.

But it's been a slow dance as well, which led us to others of like mind. Who only came to us as we were prepared to whole-heartedly receive them.

And surely we did the same steps of this jig before it seems, long ago on a far away shore. Imagine remembered bonfires burning to dimly show the way as we ducked between Shadow and Light.

Crossing every bridge, looking under each for expected trolls and vanquishing them all. Until that particular episode of the creative frenzy was spent. Yet still, thankfully the music of The Magic Of Love always lurking there inside words we wrote and spoke?

It never, ever, ends.

MICHAEL:
Fare you well. As Done is done, for now. May we, each and every one of us - forever be tangled in the wire. As we really must. Mustn't we?

TRANSIT:
Michael and Eli turn arm in arm and cross up to sit in the row of chairs among the rest of The Company.

All freeze for a slow fade down to black.

EPILOGUE

In response to the question as they shared cheroots late another night, turning his head a bit to the side yet still not quite making eye contact while obviously referencing that Then, Zackery spoke softly to Michael saying:

"Her face was tinted a pale rose, but by the moon and not from us imbibing too much wine. Which orb I haven't ever seen the same way since it had rested on her shoulders in the woods where we rambled and meandered.

"She may have thought I already had loved her much too much Before. But you must know it was never as greatly as I'd do after the coming of When. For she as my personal arsonist had set me to burn with flames never yet or since like any known in The Continuum."

Zackery took a draw on his cigar, sighed and paused as if to look away into The Ether before taking a huge draught from the wine goblet hanging almost forgotten in his left hand, then slowly continued:

"For she had broken me well most darling boy as I bled there upon the silken sheets in such an unseemingly lovely way. Silently screaming my want of only to be recreated in some startlingly new imagining of her's. And so in this manner was I raised from the ashes yet once again."

In close to slow motion Zackery wiped at the side of his face near the right eye with the back of his hand, then waved it back and forth in the air as if he had been swatting at some unseen, unheard insect instead.

"Wishing in that moment only to die in same fashion yet again in her line of innumerable times, as I already had or again would. And I watched her go to play and do and be among them. This without regard or dread of her not ever returning to my side again, for she was then as forever from our There.

"I was mostly content and not completely so both in the same instant, as I set my booted foot firmly upon the bloody step of the breath. Again preparing to timidly wade into the crimson tide while yet tethered Here by being tangled in the wire, to see just what was to be seen. So that is Why."

Now muted by the emotion of the telling, with but half of his face in the moonlight, Zackery turned at last to make direct visual connection with Michael. He openly shared an entirely wry, not weary almost-smile. And they smoked and drank in contemplative silence an immeasurably long time ...

Then Michael glances up from the desktop, roused from the concentration of his labors by the comforting rumble of a rare approaching thunderstorm. By the timepiece he is not astounded to discover that per mortal standards unfathomably innumerable hours, days or even perhaps weeks have passed since he last did so. So he'd had a goodly nap then? Oh no, for he's more awake, more alive than in a long time.

Perhaps now more so than ever before. And during such marathon, concluded by his own hand the setting down of details concerning what feels like an entire lifetime, many lifetimes, even all of our collective lifetimes - into a leatherbound volume.

He docks his exhausted pen in its always faithful holder, closing the book's use-marred cover lovingly. And pours yet another splash from the wine decanter which never runs dry, standing near to his left hand.

And there, perched on the back of his own chair is Eli. Wearing his usual rather enigmatic countenance. Having nothing further to add to the content and no additional revisions to suggest, he has for the moment again become the silently guarding Other.

Michael looks him in the eye and says:

"I remember now dearest brother. The dream, that is. It's simply about living against the black-chrome sun, is it not? Always has been and will be. As we're all perpetually tangled in the wire beneath one and inside the other. Aren't we Eli?"

"Dearest Michael, welcome past the finish line my good sir. I've been waiting, as always. And well done, as this round it's taken far less than The Keepers designated thousand years.

"Now let's kill off the last of this fine red wine here before us. And then we'll go play a play. Again. Well, perhaps after a short stroll and a long leak."

To these statements each in tandem nods a knowing yes and lifts his glass in a celebratory toast once more. Then grin mutual smiles of well-earned satisfaction at having finally completed yet another cycle of their work.

And draw deep breaths of pause to appreciate the magnificence of the purifying cloudburst, just as lightening lovingly strikes the ground not far from the Wulfsgate compound.

Insofar as the tangled wire's end can, will and must never be found by us any - they are content. At least for the moment, until beginning over again. And yet again.

And yet still, again.

AUTHOR'S NOTE

This is for my dearest most precious darling Barb, that irresistible and irrefutable force of nature. My truest desire, friend, lover, inspiration, sounding board, muse and illustrator. The very life and breath and reason for reason of me, as the only creature who ever dared put forth sincere effort to even faintly understand.

For being who and what you are to me and for having the courageous imagination to help birth the cast of characters from our collective multiple personalities and bring them kicking and screaming into what passes for the real world. For granting me the latitude to decide which would then win the sibling battles to make appearances in my work.

You have my deepest appreciation and admiration. And you own not only my heart, but my helplessly hopeful devotion until well after the end of forever. More than life kiddo, and hey I'm talking to you bird.

SOMETHING OF THEM

Greg Wood and his mate/muse the visual artist Barb Toland, fantasize living rather idyllically. Rambling and meandering from Hither to Yon, decamping from wherever they find themselves in the moment. Eons ago they were privileged to re-direct, after much time spent laboring in others' educational and computer fields.

Now most days or nights, when not pursuing individual or collaborative arts in their studio, they may often be found either sauntering along interesting trails or paddling through intriguing waterways. But always and forever tangled in the wire while chasing the path of creative dreams - which is never a short or straight line.

So there.

www.ingramcontent.com/pod-product-compliance
Lightning Source LLC
Chambersburg PA
CBHW050847180626
46814CB00007B/2662